FAMILIAR FACES, LESS FAMILIAR STORIES

FAMILIAR FACES, LESS FAMILIAR STORIES

A Collection of Short Stories

DEBAPRASAD MUKHERJEE

PARTRIDGE
A Penguin Random House Company

ISBN: Hardcover   978-1-4828-2110-9
            Softcover   978-1-4828-2109-3
            eBook   978-1-4828-2108-6

To order additional copies of this book, contact
Partridge India
000 800 10062 62
orders.india@partridgepublishing.com

www.partridgepublishing.com/india

Contents

ACKNOWLEDGEMENTS

My sincere thanks to my parents, for showing me the light of the day.

My gratitude to my wife and two daughters for bearing with all the weird manners on mine.

Thanks to Sri Ajoy Mukherjee, my uncle, without whom two of the stories would never have surfaced.

Partridge India deserves special thanks for their professional guidelines during the process of publication of this book.

Finally, my acknowledgement would remain incomplete if I fail to thank the innumerable characters that have encouraged me to sketch them.

Debaprasad Mukherjee

LOVE AND LIFE

Arindam Sarkar boarded the bus from the Esplanade Depot at about 5.30 PM. He prefers to catch the bus from the depot itself. The bus is bound to be overloaded as soon as it reaches its first stop. It is the hour of return of the office goers. Arindam prefers a seat beside the window and that's the reason he has to walk for about ten minutes from his State Bank of India office in spite of the fact that the same bus goes right through the front of his office. His residence is at Bonhoogly. It takes about an hour from Esplanade. This is, sans the infamous traffic jam of Kolkata with which you never know! This period of time is generally wasted by the commuters either in idle gossip or simply dozing the time off. The daily commuters of Kolkata are blessed with this particular quality of having naps while on move; even when standing. But that doesn't fail them to debark at their respective places. But Arindam is a little different from them. He is a seeker of a different kind. He searches for the real person within the person. Or in other words, he searches for the enlightened self behind the mask of a genuine person. He knows that a real humane quality is few and far between; but there is no harm in searching for such pearls. This zeal for life has been seen in his artistic works and photography in which he has made a little name for himself in his close circles. This positive trend of him has helped him to remain energetic at an age nearing sixty with impending retirement; much to the envy of his junior colleagues. There is nothing special in him within a small and ordinary looking frame. If one cares to have a closer look at him, he will understand that it is his vivid eyes that differentiate him from the mass.

A seat beside the window is a prize possession in a Kolkata public bus; especially in the office ending hours. That day Arindam was not lucky. As soon as he boarded the bus he found that the window seats were already occupied. He did not loss heart. There was still a preference he could opt for. He could choose the person beside whom he could take his own seat. With the long standing experience of studying human faces he could demarcate at least a decent person. The person sitting on the third seat from the front in the left side row caught his imagination. He was tall and lanky, dressed somewhat shabbily; gazing through the window with gloomy eyes and taking no interest in the surroundings. He was sitting with his long legs curled up on his seat. The man should be approximately his own age. As soon as Arindam sat beside the man he unfolded his legs and put them on the floor. Arindam was thinking. He was searching for an opportunity to start a conversation with the person and befriend him if possible. This he tries most of the times. It sometimes pays off; sometimes it doesn't. As a secondary measure he keeps a book with him which comes handy to cover up for the journey.

But the book was really not required; not on that day. The opportunity came when the conductor asked for the tickets. The man bought a ticket worth Rs. 8 against his own of Rs. 7.

"How long can you travel with Rs. 8 *dada*?" Arindam inquired. *Dada* is the common term to address a stranger in Kolkata in spite of it being meant to be 'the elder brother'.

"I really don't know. I'm new at *Kolkatta*. But I'll go up to *Rothtala*." The man answered.

In spite of the man answering Arindam's query in Bengali he had a typical North Indian accent about him which was more evident from his *Rothtala* instead of a more regular Rathtala. The same held true for *Kolkatta*. That made the task of Arindam easier.

"I guessed as much; so, you don't belong to this place?" Arindam tried to make a conversation of it.

"That is right. Although I'm a Bengali by birth, I'm born and brought up in Kanpur. It's only about a month that I've come to *Kolkatta*. I didn't want to, but it was for that damned promotion they gave me."

"You didn't want the promotion?" Arindam asked rather cautiously. He wanted to know the facts without giving the impression of intruding too much into the privacy of the man.

"The bank people are like that. I work for The Canara Bank. I didn't want the promotion. They thrust it upon me with the choice of transfer between Delhi and *Kolkatta*. Looking into it, I preferred *Kolkatta* as it is my in law's place. Do you happen to know Mr. Sanjay Roy Chowdhury of *Rothtala* by any chance? He is sort of famous in the locality. He is my father in law."

Arindam wished he knew the local celebrity. That would've endeared him more to his co passenger. But he had to admit the facts. "I'm sorry I am not acquainted with the name. But I had been to Kanpur when I was a boy. Do you know Kakadev or Geeta Nagar in Kanpur? These are the places I remember distinctly even if I stayed there long back."

The man didn't seem much interested in the geographical details of Kanpur. He was absorbed in some agony of his own. "Oh, all those places are far off from where I used to live. I was talking of banks. Do you have any idea of the apathy with which the bank employees are dealt with?"

This came as an outburst of emotion from the man. And on the flip side, Arindam, as a bank employee himself could share a sort of camaraderie with the man.

"I work with the State Bank of India. I was shuffled out to the Andaman and Nicobar Islands for some time against my will." Arindam smiled.

"There, there you are. These people treat their employees with utter disdain." There was a twinkle in the eyes of the man but it suggested more of gloom than distaste for his employers. "By the way, I'm Pinaki Lahiri." He added as an afterthought.

"Arindam Sarkar here," said Arindam in a diminutive tone as if the name didn't matter.

A hawker was selling salted groundnuts in small packets. Arindam purchased two packets and offered one to Pinaki. Pinaki accepted after moments of hesitation.

"Does your wife stay with you?" Arindam ventured rather hesitantly being fully aware that this could well be a man's Achilles Heel.

"She used to. But she has been transferred to Vishakhapattanam as well. She works for the Vijaya Bank. You know Mr. Sarkar; it is painful to stay away from one's wife, especially at our age." Pinaki started confiding in Arindam.

It is so with many people. Some couples become so much dependent on each other over the time. But there is something more to it than the plain words are suggestive of. Arindam had often seen that his sixth sense paid. "It has to be," he said in a non committal manner.

"I've got a flat at Maniktala which I had given on rent so long. But now I've given a notice to my tenant to vacate the same. Possibly they'll vacate the flat in a month or so. But what use staying in the flat all alone while your wife is working somewhere else?" Pinaki sounded remorseful.

"Of course," Arindam had started suspecting that it was yet another saga of two middle aged love birds having been separated by the circumstances. Might be his sixth sense didn't serve him well for once.

"May be you think that I'm henpecked or so, it is nothing like that," Pinaki smiled, "I love her alright; but actually it is she who provides me with the courage to sustain the loss I've undergone. She also suffers as much as me, but she doesn't show it. She is much stronger mentally than me." Pinaki made a deliberate halt.

"Don't you think all of us undergo some loss sometime or other? In case you consider me worth disclosing your pain you can share the same with me. If nothing, it will ease your suffering to some extent." Arindam sat intent and straighter.

"I'll tell you; tell everything. In fact I was searching for someone who'll understand and has the patience to listen to me."

There was a long pause before Pinaki started again. Arindam preferred to maintain silence during this period.

"It is about my son Dipankar, my only child. He was in the Army." Pinaki resumed.

The use of 'was' sounded ominous to Arindam; especially as it was correlated to the 'Army'. He shuddered without saying a word.

"He has been brilliant throughout his career. In spite of lucrative offers from corporate sectors after obtaining an engineering degree from a reputed college he preferred to join the Corps of Engineers as a Lieutenant," recounted Pinaki, oblivious to the feelings of his audience. "He loved to be seen in the olive greens. He was doing pretty well in the Army as well. After his training was completed in the Officers' Training centre he was posted at Ladakh. It happened there."

"What happened?" Arindam asked with baited breath.

"He was a favorite with his Commanding Officer. On that eventful day his CO was going out on a pleasure drive in a jeep. He loved to drive himself in such occasions. He asked Dipankar to hop in beside him. The jeep crashed after travelling some distance. His CO died on the spot. Dipankar survived grievous injuries on head and on the spine. He was rushed to Leh Military Hospital. It was then I was given information." Pinaki stopped, as if to gather some courage to continue further on.

"You must've rushed to the spot immediately," suggested Arindam who was getting engrossed in the story gradually.

"Yes, I made a move immediately for Leh along with my wife. The Army made all the arrangements for us to reach there. They arranged for the train tickets up to Jammu and from there we were taken to Leh by helicopter. They made the best possible arrangements for us. But do you know Arindam Babu; we couldn't even thank them at that time!"

"Why?"

"We had forgotten all the civilities then. I and my wife hardly talked to each other, let alone talking to them. In fact I had developed a kind of apathy for the Army that time. The only thought that occupied us was whether we would be able to see our son alive when we reached there. I don't remember what we ate or drank those days. When we reached Leh we saw our son alive, but barely."

"What condition was he in?"

"We could only have a look at him from outside the glass panel of the ICU. He was barely breathing and was fitted with all sorts of gadgets. Other than his chest heaving up and down there was no sign of life in him. Yet that was a consolation of sorts. Our boy was living!"

"Did you talk to his doctor?" Arindam asked.

"I did; but he could not provide us with much hope. We were informed that he had suffered a head injury along with fractures in seven of his spinal bones. It was the doctors' first concern to bring him back to consciousness which in itself was an arduous task. The spinal fractures were to be addressed at a later date after that."

"What happened after that?" Arindam's inquisitiveness was growing every passing moment.

"Do you believe in God?" Pinaki asked all of a sudden.

"Well, it depends on how you consider God to be," Arindam was rather cautious in his reply, "but why did you ask it?"

"I never believed in God, much to the dismay of my wife. But I think God makes one believe in Him when time comes. I prayed and prayed for three days along with my wife and our prayer was answered. Dipankar came back to full consciousness but was unable to move his lower limbs. The doctors informed that the lower half of his body was paralysed altogether. It was first time after the incidence that some form of rationality came back to us."

Arindam's eager eyes were fixed on Pinaki. The bus conductor shouted, "Sinthee junction; Sinthee junction," thereby suggesting that Bonhoogly, Arindam's stop was not far off from here.

"I think your stop is not far off. Should I stop here?" Pinaki sounded embarrassed lest he caused inconvenience to Arindam.

"That will amount to doing disfavour to me. I pray you not to stop at this point. I want to listen to everything and for that I'm willing to accompany you as long as it takes." Arindam clasped both the hands of Pinaki earnestly. He knew that he would not sleep peacefully unless he had heard all of it.

Traffic jams are generally considered as curse by the Kolkata commuters. But that day Arindam realised that it could come as a boon sometimes. It was at that point the traffic came to a standstill with no sign of improvement for an indefinite period. The vehicles switched off their ignition and the passengers started a pandemonium hurling select abuses to an array of people ranging from the traffic police to the Chief Minister of the state. Arindam however, sat more intently and listened to Pinaki.

"It was at that time they decided to operate on Dipankar for his spinal bone fractures. This was not possible at Leh hospital and he was shifted to Command Hospital Delhi by Air Ambulance. We were also carried in the same to Delhi. Arindam Babu, I must confess that the Services people have got a full-proof arrangement for everything. You can never blame them."

"And was he operated at Delhi?" Arindam enquired.

"Yes, he was; by the best possible surgeons," Pinaki continued in a melancholy tone, "but that did not bring his senses in the lower limbs back. The doctors told that the damage was permanent. But at least he could sit on his own after the surgery. He had to be on a urinary catheter regularly. It was sad; but it was better to have a disabled son than having no son at all. Don't you think so?"

A nod was the only answer that Arindam could provide.

"He was kept in the Army with full pay for a year or so. During this time another good thing happened. With proper toilet training it was possible to get rid of the urinary catheter. However, there was no further improvement in his condition. Then he was released on medical ground. I believe they have got a rule by which they have to abide."

"So where does he stay now? It must be difficult since both of you are away from Kanpur." Arindam thought that they were reaching the end of the tale.

Pinaki's face brightened all of a sudden. "He stays with none of us. He stays at Bangalore. He works there as an executive in a multinational company. He gets a handsome salary there." Pinaki smiled.

"How come he got into the job?" Arindam was rather bewildered at the fairytale turn of events.

"Oh, that? He had only lost his lower limbs; not his sharpness, neither his determination. After he came home he studied hard for a year to get admission into a management degree and cleared the CAT in the first attempt itself. He got admitted to IIM Ahmadabad."

Cracking the Common Admission Test for Management in the top institutions takes a heck of a preparation and discipline. But Pinaki's statement suggested it to be as easy as going to the kitchen garden and plucking off a couple of brinjals.

"And he got this job in the IT sector. I have reasons to believe that he is somewhere at the top of the ladder there and is well respected. Well, have you seen '3 Idiots'?" Pinaki asked, making a sudden diversion from the topic.

Arindam was acquainted with the movie '3 Idiots' which was launched not so long back. "Yeah, I've seen the movie."

"Have you seen the 'Married Students' Hostel' depicted in one of the shots?"

Arindam could not remember the shot vividly. "May be there was. I'm not sure. But what has it got to do with?"

"It was in one such hostel that Dipankar stayed while pursuing his management studies."

"But didn't you say it was a married students' hostel?" Arindam wanted to get the things straight.

"Yes I did. Dipankar was married by that time."

"You mean to say he was married early, while in the Army itself or prior to that?"

"No, he got married after the accident, while he was preparing for the exams."

"How was it possible?" Arindam made no attempt to undermine his surprise.

"It was all because of my charming little daughter in law. I knew that girl right from her childhood. They were, in fact our neighbors. Dipankar and the girl, Rima by name, used to play together and they grew up together. She is a brilliant student herself and she had already passed out from one of the business schools while Dipankar was preparing for his exams. She also had secured the job of an executive in one of the leading automobile companies by that time. One day she approached me and simply said, 'uncle I want to get married to Dipankar.' I was shocked. 'Are you out of your senses girl?' I asked. 'No uncle, I'm in my full senses. In fact this is the most sensible thing to do after what has happened to Dipankar. We decided to get married long back and then this accident occurred. Won't it amount to cheating if I step back now? And how can you desert a person you love only because he has been disabled by an unfortunate accident? Can love be that fragile? Wouldn't Dipankar do the same thing had the accident occurred to me?' I was bowled all over by that little girl at that point. I knew her all along; but I never had any idea of the magnitude of her heart. She is a Goddess to me Arindam Babu." Pinaki made a futile attempt at concealing his tears.

"How did her parents react?" Arindam asked after Pinaki had gained reasonable control over his emotions.

"I did meet her parents, Mr. and Mrs. Saxena after that. They are good people. Her father said, 'pairs are made in heaven. Who are we to distort that? Leave it to the Almighty and everything will be in its place.' Rima and Dipankar simply went to the marriage registrar and got married with both the parents as witnesses along with a few of their friends. The function that followed was simple and private affair. As far as my knowledge is concerned, they live more peacefully than most conventional couple."

"So you don't have to worry about your son now since such a devoted wife is there to look after him," quipped in Arindam, relieved to have come to a solution to the chain of events at last.

"Well, Rima has her headquarters at Bangalore; but she can't stay there for long. She has to make frequent business tours to all parts of India and away from India on some occasions." Pinaki expressed, but the expected concern was conspicuous by its absence.

"Then it must be difficult on Dipankar's part to carry out his day to day affairs?" Arindam suggested.

"Not exactly; there is a boy who looks after him and assists him in all the matters."

"Does the boy stay with him all the time?"

"Yes, that's another story. He used to be a thief some years back. Once he sneaked into our house; that was about three years back and got caught in the action. He was about eighteen that time. After getting caught red handed he resigned himself to his fate which presumably would lead to the police station or a juvenile rehabilitation centre. I was also of the opinion that he should have been handed over to the police. But Dipankar had other ideas. He offered him some refreshment and started talking to him. It came out that the boy was an orphan and that was his maiden attempt at having an individual income. He called himself Robin. From that time he stayed with us. He did the errands in our house; but he developed a particular fascination for Dipankar. Dipankar was also very fond of Robin and he educated Robin to a reasonable extent. While going to Bangalore, Dipankar wanted to take Robin along with him. We didn't deny, of course. By then, Robin knew exactly what Dipankar wanted from time to time like the back of his hand. Last time we went to Bangalore I was pleasantly surprised to see him. He has grown up into a perfect young man; smartly attired, English speaking and so on. He is being given a regular compensation of Rs. 5000 a month. In addition, he does some business from home.

Dipankar cannot stand shabbily dressed people as companion, may be a trend he has inculcated from the Army. Robin does everything to help Dipankar including cooking the meals. But Dipankar loves to do the marketing stuff himself. Almost every day he visits the market to fetch fresh vegetables and poultry." Pinaki came to a sudden stop with the suspicion that he might be stretching story too long for the tolerance level of his listener.

"Did you say Dipankar goes to market every day? But he can't walk." Arindam wanted to clarify his doubts. He wondered at marvel of the tale being unfolded at each step.

"Why only to market? He has to go to his office everyday as well. Oh, I forgot to mention; he did a favour to a renowned car company once with some electronic device development and in return the company has gifted him a specially designed car which has no use of legs in controlling it. It carries him all over Bangalore."

The standstill of traffic had come to an end finally. The bus started moving again. Arindam would get down in another few minutes. He remained speechless and kept looking at Pinaki who had turned his face towards the window; either to ascertain his debarking stop, or may be, to conceal the play of emotions running his face.

Arindam got down at Bonhoogly stop after giving a soft squeeze on the hands of Pinaki. He couldn't let out a word. Even he forgot to ask for the contact number of Pinaki. On his walk towards home he kept thinking of the tale. *What does this tale tell? It is one of grit, determination, never say die spirit and of the purest form of love. I want to let people know the story; at least the people who matter. Let it be learnt by the youth who curse their fate or the governance for their inability to make it a career without putting a bona-fide effort; let it go to the people who consider their lives doomed by destiny for the insignificant losses they have undergone; let it be known to all the young love birds who change their partners with the frequency of changing dresses on utterly trivial pleas. But I may not be that good in putting the things in words. Well, one day I'll tell the story to one of my nephews who has a penchant for literary writing; maybe he can put it up in a better way.* Arindam felt good that amongst all the turmoil of this increasingly vicious Earth there are people who make it worth living.

He pushed the doorbell of his house.

<hr />

BLOODY SWINE

It was a less than perfect winter morning. Given that it remains foggy in the early part of morning at this part of the world, it was unexpected at 10.30 in the morning. The road leading from Rourkela to Bondamunda was reasonably forlorn for such a time in the morning. The road was soggy and visibility not so great. Rourkela is the steel township in the state of Orissa and Bondamunda is an adjacent small time town mainly inhabited by railway staffs. The distance between the two towns is a little over ten kilometres. For most of the path, the roadside shops were closed. However, the shops near Diesel Colony, which marked the beginning of habitation of Bondamunda, had started opening in tandem. It was business hour for them.

And so it was for inspector Parshanath Bhoi. He was the officer in charge of Diesel Colony police station. In little more than a year he was posted in this station, he has made a good impression of himself. Well, his appearance helped. He is tall, with a proportionate horizontal expansion, dark complexioned, with darker moustaches twisted up to be at a kissing distance of the lower boarder of both his ears. The moustache and short-cropped hairs are regularly taken care of to look shiny black even at an age nearing fifty. Add to that his voice; his normal voice is often mistaken for growling. Overall, he suffices to be a typical officer in charge of a small police station. In local parlance, he is a *Daroga*. It is generally believed, as well as said aloud in his known circle that if you have to be a Daroga, you have to be one like Bhoi Daroga. They say that looks can be deceptive; but there was nothing deceptive about Bhoi. In his area, there is a regular menace of wagon breakers. Bhoi has indentified two such gangs. At the outset, he had called the leaders of both the gangs and made sure that there was a peaceful co-existence between the two. Their operative days were distributed equally with mutual understanding. And for all the pain Bhoi demanded a minor commission from both the parties. Bhoi thought he deserved the cut and the parties thought it was on the higher side. Yet a settlement was agreed upon after some bargaining at a tripartite meet. The system is running alright ever since. Not that there had not been hitches. Take the example of last month. Abdul Samad of Reddy's gang ventured to sneak a box of wristwatches from a wagon in the shed while it was the day of action by Moharana's gang. Quite naturally, Moharana's gang attacked Abdul and he lost his right arm below the elbow in the process. Daroga Bhoi rushed to the spot, admitted Abdul in the local railway hospital and put him behind the bar once the treatment was completed. And for all his pains, Bhoi charged a minor sum from Reddy as a compensation for breach of contract. Although Reddy complained the 'minor' sum to be astronomical, he had to pay it considering it a professional hazard. Then, Bhoi makes mass arrests before elections or before a VIP visit, only to release them after the occasions are over. It is a tedious job for Bhoi, which he performs to perfection. In addition, there are other complaints of theft, burglary etc. There, the modus operandi is easy. Catch hold of the culprit and strike a deal with him. If the culprit is ready to pay in cash or kind, spare him. Otherwise, put him behind the bar and go through the legal procedures. It is a win-win situation for Bhoi Daroga. Either you win in kind, or in name and fame. But it is better said than done. You have to know the thugs of your area like the back of your hand and Bhoi maintains a meticulous record of that.

However, we were talking of that misty morning. Parshanath Bhoi was returning to his police station after taking care of some errand at Rourkela. He was on his Enfield motor bike and was driving it cautiously because of the weather conditions. As he reached beginning of Diesel Colony, he started feeling like a king. It was his area after all. Here the people would salute him or would fold their hands in respect whenever he faced them. Here he does not need to pay for minor services like taking a *jarda-paan* from the betel shop or to have a haircut. His posture on the bike becomes straighter at this point and so it did on that day. It happened then, as he was taking the mild curve to his right. As he was contemplating on the tempting possibility of getting a pair of *jarda-paans* from Raghunath's betel shop, the bike slipped and he fell on the ground with all his hundred and ten kilos. At the same point, a fat hog rushed across the road making a queer sound between snorting and squeaking. Bhoi went blank for few seconds before he discovered that his nature of injury was not serious; only a few abrasions and bruises here and there. Neither his favourite Enfield bike was damaged to any serious extent. By that time, the nearby shopkeepers as well as a few commuters had gathered around the befallen inspector and his bike. There was a general air of excitement in the crowd. Police inspectors don't fall from their bikes everyday and the local shopkeepers had a feeling of rejoice within as they thought it was a god-given punishment to Bhoi for accepting all the freebies from their shop.

"Will someone lift me up instead of staring at me like fools?" Bhoi bellowed.

One of the shopkeepers lent his hand to Bhoi and another pushed him up from behind. It was no mean job to get Bhoi up. Another man did the comparatively easier task of getting the bike up on its wheels and putting it on its stand.

"Who the hell did this?" Shouted Bhoi, as he suspected a foul play in the incidence. Like a dutiful inspector, he suspected a foul play in whatever happened around him. Story goes that once he had suspected a foul play when his wife sneezed three times instead of her customary two while she woke up in the morning. He straightened his cloths. Poncha, the barber started rubbing off the dirt from his dress.

"This is unusual. Our 'Sir' passes through this road everyday and I have never seen him topple like this. There has to be some miscreant." Purnachandra, the laundry owner looked grave as he uttered these words. He was an elderly man who has seen it all.

But no suspect could be located after much discussion and some looking around.

"There must be a stone or brick somewhere in the road. I know, the truck drivers do this often as they stop on the road. I would like to see the truck driver." Bhoi at this point was standing with both his hands on his waist. He was feeling a lot better now in spite of a mild ache at his lower back.

There was a general agreement in the public that it could be the possible cause and a comb-operation was launched immediately. Unfortunately, that stretch of the road was found to be free from any possible obstructive device; no stone, no brick, no pothole, not even a pebble. Frustrated, Bhoi thought it better to sit on the bench of a tea kiosk and Jagannath, the kiosk owner started preparing a cup of special tea cursing his fate.

"What I feel, sir, there is an unscientific construction of the road at the particular turn where you lost your balance." There was a bright looking thin boy in his early twenties who approached Bhoi from the crowd.

"Who the hell are you?" Bhoi was not in a particular mood to socialise.

"Just a nobody compared to you sir," the boy scratched his head, "I am a law student studying in my second year. I just stopped over to have a cup of tea. I know of one such case in which the municipal authorities had to pay a complainant a good sum of money for faulty construction of road which caused an accident."

"Is it so?" Bhoi got interested. "You seem to be a clever guy. Why don't you sit down while we can discuss the things? Jagannath! One more 'special' for the boy."

The boy sat down on the bench alongside Bhoi. His purpose was served. He wanted to have a free cup of tea. He was no law student either. He studied engineering in the National Institute of Technology at Rourkela and was in his final year. He made it up to create an impact on the spot. "Have a good look at the side of the road sir. Doesn't the slope look steeper than the other parts?" He pointed his finger at the turn.

"Well, of course it does," Bhoi twirled his moustaches. He could not see any difference in construction of the road.

"There you are sir! Give a strong letter to the municipal office. If they don't relent, put up a case in the court. In case you need help, I can suggest you a good lawyer." The boy was fluent in his communication. The nearby shopkeepers marvelled at the ease with which the boy sat beside the powerful Daroga and was talking on equal terms. May be it was something to do with education!

"I can take care of that. But are you sure a case can be framed?" Bhoi was not very convinced.

"I am telling you sir, a case is definitely on. In the previous case I was telling you,—"

"Okay, but in case I need you, how can I find you?" Bhoi took the cup of tea from Jagannath.

"That should not be difficult. Just remember Jayant Sahu, 2nd year, Rourkela Law College. An easy name to remember, sir." The boy accepted his cup of tea as he wondered whether he was stretching the thing a bit farther than he could handle.

While sipping from the cup, Bhoi's spirit dampened to some extent. It is one thing to catch hold of a miscreant and bullshit him. But to crack down upon a government servant is a different ball game all together. There are legal hang-ups and one has to go through a long range of procedures. As an inspector, Bhoi has gone to the court several times and it was always a cumbersome thing to deal with the lawyers. Bhoi had always believed in instant decisions in which he was the judge and he was the prosecutor as well.

As soon as the tea was finished, Raghunath attended Bhoi with a pair of jarda-paan in his hand. Bhoi put these in his capacious oral cavity reluctantly and ordered for another pair which was to be packed. As Raghunath came back with the packed betel, he stood there, scratching his head. Bhoi did not like that. For a crazy moment he even apprehended that Raghunath might ask for the cost of the paan; but soon better senses prevailed. It was impossible on part of Raghunath; even after witnessing him toppling over.

"What is it Raghunath?" Bhoi asked almost benevolently.

"Should I speak something if 'Sir' allows me?"

"Go ahead."

"I saw a hog getting panicky and running across the road. May be you hit the hog and lost your balance." Raghunath was as humble as he could be.

In the pandemonium, people had forgotten about the hog. Now all of them remembered it simultaneously.

"They have no business leaving stray swine on the road," remarked Poncha, the barber.

"Right," echoed Ramlakhan, the carpenter, "is the road for commuters or is it to be used as a make-shift pig sty?"

"Is it so?" Jumped up Bhoi in excitement. "So it was a swine! I suspected as much. Does anyone know the owner of the beast? I would like to meet the person and teach him a lesson on pig-keeping." Bhoi at last found a way of reinstating his lost pride.

"It is Daduram, the sweeper sir. He is the only guy who keeps pigs in this vicinity." It was Poncha who made the declaration. He had an old score to settle with Daduram. They lived in the same slum behind the shops.

Two persons were sent by Bhoi to summon Daduram in. They returned after about ten minutes with old Daduram at their toe. Daduram looked over eighty with a frail frame and was ailing. He stood in front of Bhoi with folded hands and said, "Hazoor."

"So you are the one who keeps swine?" Bhoi burst out so loudly that the old man went into a bout of coughing. Bhoi waited patiently.

"I used to sir, until a year back. It was a part of my business." Daduram started panting. "The last of the pigs died one year back. I am too old to take care of the animals. My sons have no interest in pigs. Why should they have? One is a Gang-man in the railways and the other works in a departmental shop. I wish I had the pigs; but there is none in my possession at present."

"Then whose pig it was that occupied the road behaving as if it were its drawing room?" Bhoi had an uncanny feeling that he was coming back to square one.

Daduram was at a loss for words. Someone in the crowd explained to him that the pig had the audacity to knock down a person of the stature as high as that of Bhoi-Daroga a little while back. People in general were having a free entertainment at the cost of the event. Police officers in general and Bhoi Daroga in particular never shared a great reputation in public. Bhoi Daroga realised that he had to leave the spot soon. But he was reluctant to do so without an act of chivalry.

"Too bad of the pig to come into the way of the motorbike of his Highness," Daduram had a tone as if he was apologising on behalf of the pig community, "but there are people in other areas who keep pigs. In addition, there might be stray pigs which do not belong to anyone."

Bhoi did not have much idea on local pigs; or about any pig for that matter. He thought it better to accept whatever information Daduram passed on. The crowd seemed to be at a loss of and were devoid of any further ideas. In fact, Bhoi suspected that there might be a few faces in the crowd that were trying to conceal a smile. For a wild moment, he contemplated on the possibility of putting the pig behind the bar. Was there a law on it? He looked for the law student. He was to be seen nowhere.

Bhoi had to give up at last. He slowly walked towards his Enfield motorbike. It was one of those days; even the bike refused to buzz for a few kicks. Finally, it came to life with a desperate kick. Bhoi looked around. There was the crowd that never left the scene. He moved the throttle, looked at both his sides for a final time and uttered, "Bloody swine," and he speeded off on his way.

In the Nick of Time

Birupaksha Samaddar approached the tall stone building in the Strand Road of Kolkata near the High Court Building with tired, but steady gait. He looked up. There was the huge board on the building depicting 'State Bank of India (Local Head Office).' There was a hustle bustle of a variety of people in front of the office. There were the vendors of different kind, the passersby, the bystanders, the black coat clad lawyers and so on. Birupaksha halted near a tea kiosk for a cup of tea. The March heat of mid-day took its toll on all his eighty six years. A young man vacated his seat on a bench in the kiosk to accommodate Birupaksha. Birupaksha nodded in appreciation and rested his tall but steady lanky frame on the bench. *Courtesy has not been abolished altogether from the youth yet*, he thought and folded his old fashioned umbrella to keep it beside him. Talking of courtesy, he expected that he would get it from someone inside the building; at least some concern for his purpose. Yes, he had a purpose in coming here braving the scorching sun all the way from Lake Town. All his life he has been fond of justice and rationality and while serving in the Public Works Department of the Govt. of West Bengal till twenty six years back, he has done justice to his job in the most upright manner. His uprightness and honesty could still be marked in his wrinkled face with a strong jaw line. He entered the building with determined steps after throwing off the earthen tea cup as he finished the tea.

Birupaksha reached for the enquiry section. There was a middle aged lady sitting at the counter who seemed to take more interest in all the worldly affairs other than her own job. At that moment she was having an animated discussion with someone about which was apparently the best place to buy a *Banarasi Silk* for a prospective bride.

"Madam, Could I have a word with you?" Birupaksha asked gently.

The madam in question simply indicated her hand to wait and continued on her cell phone. "No, no Madhuri, Gariahat is the best place for bridal purchases whatever you say; may be at Shyambazar it will come a bit cheaper, but for quality and variety you must go to Gariahat. Don't you remember the last time we went to Gariahat during Sulekha's daughter's—"

"Madam, I'm coming from a long way. If you could kindly—"

The lady switched off the phone with the instruction that she would call her back later. "So, what do you want to know *Dadu?*"

Dadu is a Bengali term used for grandfather and is generally used to denote all the old men in this part of the world; Birupaksha never minds being addressed so, as is very often the case; but in this particular address he couldn't help noticing a touch of arrogance and 'how-dare-you' sort of tinge. He preferred to ignore it.

"Can you tell me where pension-complaint section is?" he asked in his polite manner.

"Oh, that? It is on the first floor, right hand side. Anyone here could have told you that."

"Thanks." Birupaksha turned towards the lift. But before he could have taken a couple of steps, he overheard the lady at the counter speaking to someone else, "Don't know where this old haggard comes from!"

Birupaksha halted and took a sudden U turn and walked back to face the lady at the counter once more. For a change he was not seen in his usual polite manner.

"And also tell me the direction of the overall in charge of this office. I would like to talk to him. What is he officially called by the way?"

"He,—he is the Ch—Chief General Manager. B—but I'm afraid you can't meet him directly." The lady seemed scared.

"I'll prefer it to be my business. Just tell me where his office is."

"On the third floor; you can see the direction as soon as you get out off the lift."

"Thanks once again." Birupaksha left the panicked lady behind and went off.

I'll rather go to the General Manager or whatsoever and talk to him straightway. There is no point talking to the junior staffs. The disdain with which they've treated me so far! And now with the behavior I received at the beginning I don't trust anyone. With these thoughts he went in the direction of the CGM's office.

The guard was dozing on a stool. But he turned out to be better person than the lady he met first.

"I'm sorry you can't meet CGM sahib now. He is busy in a meeting and it'll run till late in the evening. You can however meet Samaresh Babu, PA to the CGM, and tell him whatever you want to. You can be rest assured it will reach the CGM sahib." He told after Birupaksha approached him and ushered him to Samaresh Babu's office.

Samaresh Kundu was suave, had the looks of a philanthropist under his near bald head and behind high powered glasses. He was on the plumper side suiting his late forties.

"What can I do for you, sir?" Samaresh asked with a smile.

It pleased Birupaksha. He sat down on a chair in front of the PA's table. Another man was also seated on one of the chairs. The air conditioned room comforted Birupaksha as he started talking.

"I have retired from Bengal Govt. job twenty six years back. To be precise, I used to work for the PWD. I've been receiving my pension through your bank all these years. I am getting my pension regularly; but according to my own calculations, I'm receiving less than I am entitled to. As per my calculations, so far I've received about Rs. 45000 less."

"Didn't you inform your local bank about it?" Samaresh interrupted.

"I did; in fact so many times I approached them in last twenty years. They have failed to give any satisfactory reply. My guess is they never tried to fathom out the discrepancy."

"Which is your local branch?"

"It's the Burdwan main branch of SBI. I used to work at Burdwan and stayed back there for a long time after retirement. It is till recently I've come to stay at Kolkata and I thought I should give it a last try in your office. You see, I'm like a ripe mango hanging from its withered stalk. I can topple any day. For that matter I don't need the money that badly either. But why shouldn't I get justice before I die? You must answer my queries. I may be wrong in my calculations; and in such a case justify that and give me a reply. That's all I want." Birupaksha unfolded a few papers from an envelope and spread it over the table. "Here is the application I've made for the same and I've attached a calculation sheet of mine about the details."

Samaresh took the papers and looked into it. It contained a hand written application on plain paper with neat and bold writing, relevant pension documents and a precise calculation done on a sheet of paper ranging over all the twenty six years of him as a pensioner. Then there were the photocopies of the earlier correspondence made with the SBI Burdwan branch. There was also a landline number given in his contact address.

"You have come to the right place sir. This case merits the attention of the higher authorities. I'll make sure that your application reaches the hand of the CGM today itself. And your case will be taken up as an urgent matter. I'm sorry for the inconvenience caused to you in this regard. The Burdwan branch should've referred the case to us at a much earlier date." Samaresh was earnest in his reply.

"Well, talking of inconvenience, I had to meet a lady at the enquiry counter," Birupaksha continued rather sullenly, "who, in my opinion needs a bit of lesson in pursuing her duty as well as in the manner to behave with the strangers, especially the old ones like me. This, I think will go a long way in maintaining customer relationship in this era of privatisation of banks."

"Sanghamitra, I'm sure that is Sanghamitra. You are not the first one to have a complaint against her. She had been reprimanded earlier for this. There are a handful of people who bring bad name to the organisation. There are people like that in every organisation. Don't you agree?" Samaresh said.

Birupaksha nodded. He still remembered the rotten lot in his own department.

"This will be reported sir; my sincere apologies to you on behalf of the office." Samaresh reassured Birupaksha.

Birupaksha came out of the office of the PA.

The LHO or the Local Head Office of the State Bank of India is a busy one. While being located at Kolkata, it supervises all the banking actions of the Bengal Circle as well as that of the Andaman and the Nicobar Islands. The Chief General Manager is in overall charge of the office. He is assisted by two General Managers; namely, GM 1 and GM 2 who are responsible for different sections. The pension section was under the jurisdiction of GM 2. The application of Birupaksha was put up to the CGM on the day following the one he had handed it over to his PA. The first instinct of the CGM Mr. Subramanium was to direct it to the GM 2. Then he thought otherwise. The official process might delay the matter a little more. Instead, he called for Reddy. Tushar Reddy was the Deputy General Manager in the Complaint and Grievance section. Reddy had come from the ranks of bank and not only does he know his job inside out, he loves banking. His zeal for banking and customer dealing had been extraordinary. That's why he is in that section. Whatever might be the problem of the customer; whether they contact by telephone or personally, the job was assured to be done. And the best thing was, no customer returned unsatisfied. Take the example of a week back. An old man came for some arrear receipt of his pension. He came from a remote village of Bengal. The clerk at the counter found out some irregularity in his papers and informed him that it would take another month or so to be processed by the bank. Undone, he approached Reddy. Reddy though of Andhra origin, has stayed in Bengal since last two generations and has practically become a Bengali. Before the man could utter a word, Reddy realised that the man was tired and hungry and took him to the canteen, offered him snacks and tea. He listened to his complaints in the canteen itself and decided that it could be solved within an hour. The old man got his cheque on the same day. *Who would not be pleased by such service!* Subramanium thought. There were many such stories doing the rounds in the office. May be there were some Subramanium didn't hear of. *Pity that Reddy will retire in a year!* Subramanium suppressed a forthcoming sigh.

Tushar Reddy is a busy man. The bank has given him so many things; the power to run a family decently, a shelter over his head and above all a reputation in the society. He believes that there is no harm in paying something back to the bank. This is especially so in the era of mushrooming of private banks. He cannot bear any bad name to the SBI. He has written about it in the bank chronicle, he has tried to make an efficient team of the boys working under him; but the trend with the younger generation has looked ominous. They look at it like any other job without any emphasis to qualities like empathy, sincerity and so on. Tushar has given up. But one thing is certain; the only year he is left with the job, he will not let his bank down.

Portly Tushar was doing exactly the same thing in his cell. With his short height, pot belly and plump torso he gave the appearance of one from a comic character. Add to that his crew cut salt and pepper hair and white handle bar moustache. But contrary to what his appearance suggests, he moves very fast and has a knack of finishing his job in the minimum time possible. That day he was talking to a particularly stubborn customer in his land phone at the office.

"Sir, we are taking utmost care to settle your home loan as fast as possible. You need to have no worry whatsoever." Tushar told the customer over the phone.

"I have been listening to your cock and bull stories since a month. I think I did a mistake in not applying for the loan from HDFC bank. The others who did so have got their loans sanctioned much before." The customer grumbled at the other end.

"Mr. Sen, I can assure you that you made the right choice. There is no hidden cost with us and your rate of interest is going to be much lesser with us." Reddy was as smooth as silk.

"And that's why you make it a point to drag the thing as long as you can!" Mr. Sen was still fuming.

"Well sir, when do you have to make your first payment to the builder?" Reddy never lost his temper.

"In a week's time at the most. If I don't get the cheque during that period, not only do I forfeit my claim to the house; you face a trial in the consumer court as well."

"How about paying us a visit day after tomorrow and collecting your cheque?"

"In that case, I'll meet you with a box of sweets." Mr. Sen showed signs of melting.

"Please do come the day after tomorrow at 11 AM sharp and your cheque will be ready at the counter. And by the way, no sweets please; just send me a card for the opening ceremony of your house." Tushar Reddy was smiling; *it is a pleasure to have a contented customer.*

"Sir, you have been so helpful; I in fact, regret the way___"

Tushar disconnected the phone. He had other jobs to do. Another phone was ringing. It was the intercom.

"Subramanium." It was in monosyllable from the boss himself.

"Yes, sir!" Reddy also is a man few words when it is required.

"Unless you are too busy, will you mind meeting me now? It is sort of urgent."

"I'll be there within no time." Reddy hung off. He knew that his boss meant business whenever there was a mention of urgency.

Subramanium handed over the application and the attached papers of Birupaksha Samaddar to Tushar Reddy as he entered the room. As always, he was dressed in all white over his mahogany body and there was the perpetual pattern on his forehead made of sandalwood paste. "You can go through the details at your convenience, but the gist of the matter is the man is searching for justice since quite some time and has not been able to get the same at a ripe age of eighty six. Isn't it a shame?"

"I can feel for the person, sir. And what name the bank is going to earn in such cases!" Tushar nodded solemnly.

"That's the precise reason I called for you. There can be no better person to look into the matter. Samaresh has met the person. You can gather any finer details from him if you want."

"I'll do the best I can." Tushar left the room with this assurance.

Tushar peeped into the room of Samaresh Kundu. He was alone in the office.

"Hello Mr. Kundu!" Tushar addressed as he entered the office.

"Why, it is Reddy-da!" Samaresh was pleased to see Tushar. Tushar was friendly to all the staffs in the office and he loved being suffixed 'da', or elder brother rather than the officious 'sir'. "What brings the savior of all to this humble office? Wait, let me have a guess; is it about the Birupaksha Samaddar case?"

Reddy looked at the application in his hand and gazed right at the bottom of the page. Indeed it was the name. "I guess so;" he smiled, "you have an analytic mind alright. How did the man look like?"

"Tall, thin frame and with an air of self respect."

"What was the precise nature of the problem?"

"As per his own calculations, he has been receiving lesser amount than he is entitled to all these years, and the local branch is turning a deaf ear to his pleadings."

"As usual," Reddy was remorseful, "I wonder why the local branches can't contact us straightway in case of disputes?"

"Because there is a world of difference between Tushar Reddy and other bankers; in any case, what I feel, the boss has got a sentimental interest in the case. He wants this case to be solved as early as possible along with careful handling of the case." Samaresh winked at Tushar.

Tushar took an envelope from the table of Samaresh; put the documents of Birupaksha in it and marked PRIORITY on it and went out before putting it into his briefcase on return to his own cell. He got emerged into his job once again answering phone calls and attending to the aggrieved customers.

Tushar Reddy hardly deviates from his daily routine. That evening he returned to his flat at Kasba in South Kolkata, had a bath and changed over to his pajamas and vest after pouring in talcum powder all over his plump body. Then he had a cup of refreshing strong coffee and lit a cigarette. This was only his third cigarette of the day. His doctor has put a ban on his erstwhile smoking habit of a packet a day due to his increasing cholesterol level. Then he relaxed on the armchair with the newspaper. Wife Sujatha would now be busy with her cooking and soap operas for a couple of hours. Son Srikant works for a private farm and he would be late to return. He looked at the paper. The headlines comprised of some blame game between the political rivals. He hated this type of news. For that matter, most news items are disgusting. Murder, theft, burglary, terrorism and things like that. *I wonder where the country is heading to!* He turned the pages. His eyes got stuck at a news item in one corner of the third page: **Age no bar for learning**. An 85 year old man had done is post graduation in Political Science as a private candidate from a university in Rajasthan. Seemingly it was his second post graduation from the same university. The first one he did in Sociology three years' back. Tushar liked the zeal in the man. *May be he wanted to be a post graduate in his young age but the circumstances forbade him to do so. Fancy he must be having a good brain at this age. 85 is old enough. Hold on; I've to deal with the case of a man who is of the same age; 85 or is it 86? Let me go through his papers.*

Tushar extinguished his cigarette and stashed it in the ashtray. He took out the envelope marked PRIORITY and opened it. A bunch of papers were clipped neatly together. At the top there was the hand written application in clear handwriting. He smiled to himself. He has seen that the elderly people do not believe much in modern gadgets. He himself is fond of handwritten applications. *Well, I can also be counted in the elderly group.* The application was written in simple English about how, according to his own calculations, he was getting lesser amount as pension all the twenty six years after his retirement and all his futile efforts at getting an answer from the local bank. The application ended with sentimental words like whether he deserved to get some justified reply at the fag end of his life. It was signed with the full name of Birupaksha Samaddar underneath it. He used to be a PWD officer with the Govt. of West Bengal in Burdwan District. There was a contact number given at the end along with a Kolkata address. The next page was devoted to a meticulous calculation of how he had been deprived of an amount of Rs. Forty five thousand. The other papers comprised of his pension sanction papers and the earlier correspondence he made with the bank authorities. Tushar looked at the clock hanging on the wall. It was 8.25 PM only. There was no harm in making a call to the person at this hour. He rang up the number given at the end of the application.

The bell rang for quite some time before someone answered, "Hello." It was a clear and heavy voice.

"Can I speak to Mr. Birupaksha Samaddar?" Tushar Reddy was as gentle as possible while speaking in clear Bengali.

"I am Birupaksha Samaddar. May I know what job you have with me?" Birupaksha's voice was calm and yet there was an authoritative note in his voice.

"Good evening sir, I am talking on behalf of the SBI, Local Head Office in response to your application given to us yesterday."

"Nice to hear from the bank so soon; I really didn't expect a response this early. But why 'sir'? I hate to be called 'sir.' In our time it was used as an ornamental address used by the British. Is it necessary to stick to it? How old are you, in case you don't mind?"

"I will be retiring from service next year." Reddy smiled.

"Good; in that case you can call me *dada* although I'm a bit too old to be called your elder brother as well. But since it is a general address hope you will not object to it."

Reddy was pleased. He himself was not keen on the sir-ing business.

"I will be privileged to call you dada. And it is our duty to serve the customer in the best possible way. That's why I would like to clear a few queries of mine." Reddy was not highly rated in the banking circle for no reason.

"You seem to be a decent person to me. At my age I can know a person even by his voice. Won't you tell me your name?" Birupaksha was softened in his stand.

"I am Tushar Reddy, Deputy Manager in the complaint cell of the LHO." Tushar said.

"Reddy! You must be from the South. How come you speak such fluent Bengali?" Birupaksha seemed surprised.

Tushar laughed aloud. He had to face this question many a time in his life.

"Birupaksha-da, I am as much a Bengali as you are. I am born and brought up in Bengal and grew up on the same diet of Rabindranath and Saratchandra as you have," he said.

"I didn't doubt your integrity though," Birupaksha laughed at the other end too, "I was just curious. Now what is it you want to know from me?"

Reddy liked this easy atmosphere while dealing with the parties. "You retired from Burdwan District as you have mentioned in your application."

"Yes, from the Burdwan town itself."

"Do you still reside at Burdwan?"

"No, I've left Burdwan for good about six months' back. Now I stay at the Lake Town area in Kolkata. It's my younger brother's place."

"Any particular reason for leaving Burdwan? This is not official; I'm just asking as a younger brother of yours; that is, if you consider me to be one." Reddy sounded almost apologetic.

The old man didn't seem to mind. "It's nothing much to conceal; but it might be painful on your part to listen to it. I had a good house at Burdwan where I stayed with my wife and only son. My wife died about ten years back. My son couldn't study much because of his persistent kidney ailments. However, he got a petty job with a builder and was pulling on somehow. He didn't get married either. Three years' back he was diagnosed to be a case of some cancer of kidney and his condition deteriorated day by day. I tried my best and consulted the topmost specialists, but could not_____" Birupaksha's voice choked.

"I'm sorry dada; you don't have to tell if you don't want to." Tushar felt bad for the man.

"No, listen to it. I'll feel relieved by telling it to you. Somnath, my son, died six months back. It was then I decided to sell my house there and settle in Kolkata. My younger brother had also died by that time and his widow was living in this house with their only daughter. So I decided to settle here so that I can die amongst my relations. Did I do the right thing Tushar?"

"Of course you did, dada."

"I sold my house of Burdwan for eleven lakh rupees. It was worth much more than that and people took me to be a fool. But that was about the amount I required as I borrowed some money for the treatment of my son. There is no use of any extra money at my stage. Can you say what I'll do with money?" Birupaksha sounded like a saint.

"Truly said dada; but with due apology, are you in any particular financial trouble now as you have put your papers for miscalculation of your pension?"

"No, I really don't care whether I get any money out of this. I've been making petitions to answer my queries and had been denied one throughout these years. It is a matter of principle. I may be wrong in my calculations; maybe I am to get no money after you recalculate it, but simply convey the same to me and I will be satisfied." Birupaksha panted a little.

"You give me just three days at the most dada. I'll try my level best to give a satisfactory reply to your questions. Thanks for talking to me." Reddy hung up.

The next day happened to be Saturday. It is half day for the bank. Tushar Reddy swiftly finished some of his pending works. Then he opened the calculation sheet given by Birupaksha. He could not find a flaw in it. But that was not enough. To verify the calculations they are to send the papers to the CPPC, Central Pension Processing Cell. If everything goes fine, the reply is expected by a week or so. *I have to find a way to shorten the procedure. The official information may get delayed, but there is no harm in collecting the information personally. Most of them at CPPC are known to me, but would they yield if I asked for an inside information informally? After all they also have to abide by the official rules.* Then it came to him in a flash. Biplab, Biplab Majumdar! He is the right person to approach for this. He was the same batch as Reddy in the bank and got trained together when appointed as clerks at the beginning of their service. A very efficient and jovial chap. He helped Reddy in another pension discrepancy case a couple of years ago. Then there was no communication between them. He however had the cell no. of Biplab saved. Reddy gave a call.

"Hey Tushar! Hearing after a long time. Is everything alright?" Biplab's warm voice was heard at the other end.

"I'm fine. Are you still in the CPPC?" Reddy asked.

"Well, they couldn't find a better gutter to dump me yet. Seems you are stuck with some pension complaint once again."

"Right you are. This time it is a grand old man who claims that he has received about forty fine thousand less so far. I need your help."

"Oh, you know these pensioners; most of the time they miscalculate it and harass our section with it. But since you rang up, I can smell two things; it is important and it can't wait. Am I right?" Biplab guffawed at the other end.

"I must congratulate you on your intuition. You are spot on. I have reason to believe that the man may be right. Could you spare some time for me today?" Reddy sounded earnest.

"Same old Tushar! You haven't changed an iota. But that's why I admire you. I will be there till you come and you are assured of hot *samosas* followed by tea; but you have to hurry. The babus over here are in a hurry to leave on Saturdays and in that case I'll not be able to catch hold of the concerned file."

That shouldn't be a problem. CPPC is at the junction of the Vivekananda Road and Central Avenue; hardly seven to eight kilometers from here. It is 11.45 AM now and if I take a bus from here it will take me to that office by quarter to one at a conservative estimate. Reddy stood with a start. He could have visited CPPC on Monday at his convenience. But something within him urged him to go the same day. He couldn't help being impulsive at times but he didn't mind it either.

There is a democratic way of protesting the things you don't like. That's how the political rallies and slogans had started. Tushar could not say how or when it started at all; but he could say with certainty that this was a regular phenomenon in the daily life of Kolkata. Very often it plagued the daily routine as it did that day. As soon as he stepped outside he saw a political rally centered right at the junction of the road, thereby blocking all the traffic movement. There was a dhoti clad leader delivering some igniting speech to a few hundreds of flag and poster flourishing political workers. The traffic and the traffic police alike had come to a standstill. Tushar asked a by-stander, "How long will it take to clear up the mess?"

"It has just started, dada; I reckon it will take three to four hours in the least." The man said dispassionately.

Don't think I can make it today, Tushar thought. But then he saw in his mind's eye Birupaksha saying with a wry smile, 'so, you told me that you'll be ready with a reply in three days' time! You bank people are all the same. Anyway, who cares for an old person with one step already in the grave! Thanks still.'

No, I can't let that happen. I have to do it, today itself. He saw a young man walking fast on the street. He followed him and caught up with him. "Where do you think you are going?" Reddy asked.

"My mother is sick and ailing in the hospital. She needs me urgently. I can't wait for the traffic standstill to end; it might be too late by then. The hospital is about six kilometers from here. And there are rallies at every junction over here. I'll have to walk and walk fast." The young man rushed on his way.

There lies the answer; I have to walk all the way. May be I can't walk as fast as him, but it will take me to the destination alright. Tushar made another call to Biplab requesting him to bear with him a little further and started walking. He was not accustomed with long walks for quite some time but he continued with a purpose. He perspired hard and yet enjoyed the effort. That X factor dragged him on.

Tushar Reddy reached CPPC at 1.50 PM. He was panting as he knocked the door adorned with the plate: 'Biplab Majumdar, Dy. Manager.' The entire office building had a vacant look about it. But the ever reliable Biplab was there, all smiles to receive Tushar.

"My guess is you had to walk all the way. And I made Sudhangshu and Chhotelal wait exclusively for you." Sudhangshu and Chhotelal were the junior clerk and peon of Biplab's office respectively.

"You did a great job as usual. I was half afraid that I might miss the show today; but with you at the helm of affairs_____"

"Okay, enough of back slapping. Now have some rest while we take care of the samosas and tea. Chhotelal,_____"

"I perfectly understand sir," the peon was off in a flash before Biplab could finish his words.

Over the next few minutes the two colleagues remained absorbed in personal conversation over the snacks and tea. Finally Biplab came to the point.

"Now hand me over the papers."

Tushar handed over the same and Biplab looked into it intently.

"Birupaksha   Samaddar—PWD—Burdwan—1986—hmm—let me recollect—that should be in the fifth rack, 2nd or 3rd shelf as far as I can remember," Biplab was humming in a low tone; that was his style. "Sudhangshu Babu, will you mind looking for it? Remember, 2nd or 3rd shelf, fifth rack from left." This time he said aloud.

Sudhangshu returned with the file in hand within a few minutes. "It *was* on the 3rd shelf sir!" He declared with the passion of an assistant who had seen his detective decoding a vital clue.

Biplab ignored him and kept turning over the pages in the file and stopped on a particular one. He frowned for a while and caught hold of his calculator and started running his fingers over it. The entire process took a quarter of an hour while the other three persons in the office kept looking quietly at the face of the man in charge.

Finally he gave Tushar a look of rejection. "This Birupaksha man of yours is an oaf. He doesn't know the basic calculations."

Tushar's heart sank. "That means he doesn't get anything more from the bank in the form of pension?" He told with remorse.

"Not exactly," Biplab's eyes twinkled a little, "there was a miscalculation alright; he will not receive forty five thousand bucks, instead he will receive an amount of Rs. Ninety thousand from the bank."

This was an absolute shocker. "Biplab, are you sure he will get Rs. 90,000 from the bank?" Tushar asked.

Biplab tapped on his own chest. "Once Biplab Majumdar has made a calculation, it stays calculated. You can tell your man the same from my side and let him rejoice. The formalities will take about ten days to be completed though."

Tushar Reddy got up. "I will inform Mr. Samaddar of the same, but I doubt how much he will rejoice." He left the room leaving a bewildered Biplab behind.

Sunday mornings are reserved for various personal errands. Tushar Reddy got up leisurely, had a late breakfast, went to the market, had a haircut and finally discovered that he was late for the lunch. After having a shower and lunch a short nap seemed practicable. So it was not before four in the afternoon he could dial Birupaksha at Lake Town. It was a female voice that answered his call.

"Madam, can I talk to Birupaksha Samaddar? I am calling on behalf of the bank?" Tushar clarified.

"If I'm not mistaken, you are Mr. Reddy." The elderly female voice said.

"That's right madam."

"He is my late husband's elder brother. The other day he praised you a lot. He believes that you are the person who can give an answer to his long standing grievance. Let me tell you one thing brother; he has suffered a lot in his life. Please solve his problems if you can. It has become more of a mental thing than a financial matter." The lady at the other end seemed concerned. "If you can give me your number I'll tell him to call you back. He has gone out for a stroll"

Tushar gave his number. "It is precisely for that I wanted to talk to him. I'll wait for his call."

The telephone bell rang after fifteen minutes. It was Birupaksha.

"Tushar; I hope I can call you Tushar, did you make an inquiry into the matter?"

"Dada I did; I went to the central pension section personally and got it verified," Tushar was full of enthusiasm.

"And what did you find?"

"There was indeed a mistake in calculating your pension so long. You are to receive an arrear of 90,000 instead of 45,000 as you had calculated." Tushar waited expectantly to listen to the customary gush of excitement from the other end.

But there was none. "This is what I wanted. I told you to inform me even if I was wrong. Now you have informed me that I'm wrong; even if it is more than what I calculated. Or else I'd have died with the feeling that I'd been deceived of my right while drawing pension. Thanks a lot."

"But dada, the regret letter from the bank along with your cheque will take a little while to reach you. Would you like these to be sent to your present address?"

"Now it doesn't matter how long it takes to reach me. I'm satisfied with whatever you've told me. Words from my younger brother are much more valuable to me than dumb official papers. However I'll be available in this present address of mine." Birupaksha cut off the line.

In spite of his busy schedule Tushar Reddy tried his best to get the cheque processed, yet it was on the eighth day he succeeded in getting the account payee cheque. *Tomorrow I'll type a regret letter and along with that I'll dispatch the cheque at its rightful address.* Reddy was happy that justice had been done at last.

That evening he felt a strong urge to talk to Birupaksha. He had developed sort of a bond with the person. Moreover, he had a valid background to talk to him.

"May I know who speaking?" It was a young feminine voice from the other end.

"It is Tushar Reddy from the State Bank of India. I intended to talk to Birupaksha Samaddar. We have processed the arrear cheque from the bank."

"I'm his niece. He is the elder brother of my father. My name is Shyamali. But I'm afraid it will not be possible for you to talk to him."

"Any particular reason?"

"He has left us."

"Has he left for Burdwan? I can contact him there if you give me the number."

"Possibly I couldn't make myself clear; he has left for his heavenly abode. He died last Wednesday."

"Oh my God! How did it happen?"

"That evening he was sitting in the armchair watching TV news. He asked for a cup of tea. When I handed the cup over to him, he suddenly collapsed and he did not give us the time to take him to the hospital____" Shyamali's voice got drowned in her sob.

Tushar felt that he had lost a family member of his own. Yes, it was a personal loss. He was old enough. It was bound to happen someday or other. If only the cheque and the letter could reach the man in time! Now there would be some legal jugglery to find the rightful heir to hand over the same. But pondering over the matter he found that he did not do a bad job either. He had responded to his queries and he could provide a satisfactory reply to the person before he died. Yes, just in the nick of time!

———◈———

CHRONIC

"Dad! What is 'chronic'?" my twelve-year-old daughter asked. She was going through one of her textbooks.

"Are you reading about some illness?" I asked sipping from my coffee mug.

"How did you know?" she was surprised.

"Dads are supposed to know," I said with an authoritative air. It is a different thing that as a medical doctor I am well versed with things like 'acute' and 'chronic'. However, my little girl was impressed.

"The term 'chronic' refers generally to a long standing illness or a bad habit difficult to give up. However, it can loosely be applied for anything constant, ceaseless, deep-rooted or habitual." I was in a mood to elaborate. Ruchi, my daughter, was not so impressed this time by my span of knowledge. She had her purpose served and concentrated on her book once more.

"Talking of 'chronic', I am reminded of an interesting character." I went on a reminiscence mode.

Ruchi takes some interest in my special characters. This seems more pronounced when she is studying. It was just the beginning of the evening of Saturday. Tomorrow is a holiday. I thought there would be no harm done if a class seven girl missed her studies for one evening. Ruchi closed her book and looked at me expectantly. I was surprised to notice an addition to my audience. Rajni, my better half joined the room with a plate of sizzling onion *pakodas* in a large plate. The atmosphere thus created, I began.

"Samir Bhowmick was three years' senior to me in the medical college. He was called 'chronic'." I believe in putting first thing first.

"Another of your medical college characters!" Put Rajni rather cynically.

I cannot keep these characters at bay. They keep surging into my memory lane. But it was not the moment to rue over the issue and I continued.

"Samir Bhowmick was from Tripura. He was short, frail and had a great gift for pantomime and mimicry. People loved him whenever he occupied the stage in our college auditorium. I still remember some of his specials; like 'ladies badminton' and 'a journey by a harrowed commuter in a crowded bus' amongst his pantomimes and 'the speech of Indira Gandhi', our Prime Minister that time, in his mimicry. He made several encores of these on public demand. Whenever he was at action, there were regular cheers from the audience in the form of loud shouts of 'chroni-i-i-c'. The word 'chronic' used to egg on Bhowmick-da. The term was coined by one of his classmates, Sridharan. He was also the president of our 'Menty-Club.'"

I was expecting some queries to prop up from my audience and paused at this juncture. This also facilitated the way for passing down a couple of pakodas to my mouth.

"I've never heard someone being cheered with such a queer adjective." It was not exactly an enquiry, as was expected from Rajni; she likes to put an opinion rather.

"Well," I hesitated a little, "Bhowmick-da tried his heart out at whatever he did. At the same time, he got chronically addicted to the same. It all started with liquor, which he started taking right from his first year. He boozed to glory and was named Chronic-Bhowmick. It was during one of those boozing sessions his talent in pantomime and mimicry was discovered. He performed in our auditorium and became chronically addicted to his skills. He performed in many other forums in addition to our college."

"Did you always call your seniors 'dada' or elder brother in your college days?" quipped in Ruchi, who was listening intently.

"That was the norm. We were a bit old fashioned in our student days," I admitted.

"What is this 'Menty-Club' of yours?" Ruchi was not finished yet.

"Good question," I nodded, "it was founded and organised by Sridharan. He was the self-proclaimed president of the club as well. I was not a member of the club though. It required some special talent to be included in the club."

"Like?"

"It's difficult to explain. Someone needed to have a special mental bug to be included in the club. You cannot get yourself included. You are to be picked up. For example, let's take the case of Prashant Mishra. He was in 2nd year then. We were dancing on the occasion of New Year eve. Prashant could not dance and he never had taken an interest in that either. In spite of our repeated cajoling, he stood aside. Then he sat on a wooden chair lying over there. All of a sudden, he started dancing and that too better than any of us. He was rhythmic and was a great sight to look at. After he stopped about ten minutes later, we asked how he got motivated. 'I don't know. But it all started after I got a prick from one of the protruding nails in the chair,' he said. That day itself, he was recorded as a 'Menty' and later went on to give dance performance in the auditorium. Then there was Subrat Rai. He was keeping wicket for 3rd year in the inter class cricket match between third and final year. He used to be an excellent wicket keeper as such. A ball sneaked back from one batsman and Subrat jumped in the air to catch it. He shouted 'howzzat' and looked at the umpire. The umpire was signalling four runs. As Subrat looked at his right hand glove, he saw that he had caught a flying wasp instead. Sridharan-bhai rushed to the spot to hand him over a Menty membership card."

As Ruchi started laughing, Rajni said, "Your Chronic-Bhowmick must have been a member of the club."

"Goes without saying," I said with a chuckle.

"What happened to him afterwards?" Ruchi was eager to get back to the original story.

"Nothing much except him loitering and performing in his own way. We used to meet sometimes at an occasional teashop or a cigarette kiosk. He was my senior and we did not stay in the same hostel either. Yet he seemed to like me. Once I was having my evening cup of tea in a shop with my friends. I was at the end of our second year. Bhowmick-da entered the shop alone. He looked devastated. 'Prabhat,' he said, 'can you come with me at once?' I got up and we settled down in a cosy country liquor shop after walking for about half an hour."

"So you were at those things right from your early days!" Rajni remarked diabolically.

I admit that I take an occasional drink or two at times even these days. That is never to the limit of incrimination. Yet Rajni does not miss out whenever there is an opportunity to sting. I digested it coolly.

"Mom! We can do without your penetrating comments. Please continue with your story dad. What happened in the country liquor shop?" Ruchi came to my rescue.

"Bhowmick-da ordered for a bottle of country liquor. 'I feel wretched. Final MBBS results are out and I have failed. I want to get drowned in liquor tonight,' he announced. He kept drinking and kept talking. 'I've disgraced my family,' he said. And continued speaking about how respected and how well placed his family was at Agartala. We knew that he was from a well-to-do family, and nothing beyond that. 'My father thought that I will be a great doctor and treat the needy people. We don't need money; our family has got a lot of it you see,' he said, 'all I was required to do was to make them proud. And "proud" indeed I've made them with my achievements.' He started crying."

"You must have tried to soothe him," observed Ruchi.

"I did, but not with good outcome. He developed a sudden urge to gulp beer over and above country liquor, and we moved to a bar, this time in a rickshaw. By the time we moved out of the bar, he drank too much and vomited several times on his way back to campus by a rickshaw. I had to hand him over to the safe custody of his friends in his hostel. As I started out of his room, he called me back and said, 'Prabhat, is there any point in continuing with such a wretched life?' I did not know when I started taking him seriously. I said, 'Bhowmick-da, you are known as chronic; and you know why it is. Can't you develop a chronic love for studies? Rest everything is going to be in place.' I am not sure whether he understood. He pointed his index to me with a smile and started chanting 'chronic, chronic' before he dozed off.'

"Now don't say me that he started studying seriously after that." Rajni was as cynic as ever.

"The fact of the matter is, he did," I smiled, "not only did he start studying, he got chronically addicted to studies. He succeeded a lot as a doctor in later part of his life. But that does not mean he became a 'good boy' ever after. He continued with his affairs with alcohol as well as drugs. Only his stage shows reduced in number because of paucity of time."

"What happened then?" Ruchi asked.

"He passed his final MBBS after six months with good marks to his credit. The day he passed, he caught hold of me once more and said, 'I am happy. I have passed. Now let's have some drink.' And the same sequence of events; country liquor followed by beer followed. Only difference being, the mood was cheerful. While returning to the campus, he vomited again. This time around, however, he begged me to stay in his room for sometime before I left.

I asked him, 'Did you send information to your folks back home of your result? They must be happy with the percentage you have obtained.' He remained ponderous for some time before he answered. 'I hope so,' he said, 'but I am not sure how long the happiness is going to last.' 'What is it this time?' I wondered. He smiled in a queer fashion. 'Do you think they are going to adore me if I break the news that I want to marry a prostitute?'

This was something going tangentially over my head. 'May be you drank too much,' I suggested. 'Remember Prabhat, I am chronic. I don't loss my head over alcohol,' he looked straight into my eyes, 'Her name is Sulochana. I first met her in a red light area in Calcutta one year back. You may hate me for going to a prostitute, but that does not matter. What matters is, I got addicted to the girl, chronically, as usual. I have met her several times in the mean time and discovered that she is no way different from any other girl. Ill luck mixed with an aberration of idea has led her to this profession. She had some basic education and on my urging, she has done her graduation in private as well. But that is not going to soften my old man. They are too conservative.' I could realise that. If I, who take pride in my modern ideas, cannot accept the situation within my heart, I could imagine the plight of his old father. 'I have heard that it is very difficult to get rid of prostitution for a girl even if she wants to.' I surfaced my doubts gathered from my knowledge of novels of which I was an avid reader. Bhowmick-da brushed it aside with a wave of his hand. 'These are easy to adjust my dear Prabhat. Only you have to spend right sums in right places. That has been taken care of.'

I left his hostel late at night with a dizzy head"

Ruchi was not sure what to speak at this point. She knew what a prostitute was; thanks to the movies she devoured. Rajni was sitting with a solemn face. I wondered what was on my way. But I was surprised at her next quote.

"Hats off to your Chronic-Bhowmick! It needs some guts to do a thing like that. A girl's life is always difficult. No harm is done if they had reached such a decision." She is an upright feminist whenever the occasion permitted. "I hope they got married."

"They got married alright," I nodded. "It was a private affair in a marriage registrar's office. I could not be there as a witness as I got busy with my exams. His entire family shunned him for being so obstinate in getting married to Sulochana. As far as I know, they had quite a tough time for a couple of years after his marriage."

"Did not you meet him after that?" Ruchi had found her voice again.

"I met him about three years after his marriage. They had just started seeing better days that time. Bhowmick-da had done his post graduation in internal medicine from one of the Calcutta medical colleges and was serving in a Ramakrishna Mission hospital. They had rented a house in the Phoolbagan area. Their daughter was two years' old; quite a cuddly baby."

"What about his 'chronic' habits?" Rajni asked.

"These are difficult to die," I forced out a smile, "at least with people like Samir Bhowmick. He loved boozing all right, but hardly had time for that. However, we had a quiet drink together. During the conversation, I came to know of his other chronic addictions that he had developed of late. He provided free medical advice in the evening in one of the local slum areas. In the process, he got addicted to the day to day life of the people over there; so much so that, he used to bear the schooling expenses of a few children of the area.

'May be your Chronic-da will put up his candidature in the forthcoming municipal elections,' joked Sulochana-boudi, his wife. She seemed to enjoy this chronicity of character of her husband."

"They seem to be married happily," opined Rajni.

"As far as my knowledge went, they were better clicked than most other couple I knew; but I hardly am good at understanding such things," I admitted. "But in one corner of his heart Bhowmick-da nurtured a deep routed sorrow. He missed his ancestral house. 'I wish I could be in Agartala,' he said. 'My parents failed to realise what an asset their daughter-in-law is. After my marriage, I went once to that house with Sulochana. They did not even allow us to enter the house. After Deepti was born, I sent them a message. They ignored it; I think vanity came in their way. It is only Shobhan, my younger brother who visits me at times, albeit without the knowledge of my parent.' That grief of his was compensated to some extent by his lovely daughter, I expect."

It was dinnertime. Rajni wanted to serve dinner and the rest of the story to be told at the dinner table. However, Ruchi did not want an interruption in the flow of story. "No harm is done if we take dinner a little late today," she told. Rajni had to relent.

"There is not much of story left though." I was hardly in a mood to continue. But Ruchi was not one to give up so easily.

"Where does 'Chronic uncle' live now-a-days? His daughter must be grown up by now. Did his parents accept his marriage later?" she put up a barrage of questionnaire.

I was afraid of this. The inevitable questions have come and I was to face the truth. "He is no more in this world. He died three years' back." I sighed.

Once in our school days, our English teacher was explaining what a 'tragedy' was. In that context, he had said, "Your father dies, it is not a tragedy; your mother dies, it is not a tragedy; your sweetheart dies, neither is it a tragedy. But when the hero or the heroine of a novel or a movie dies, it is a tragedy." Now I saw the effect of tragedy striking my couple of audience. They remained dumb. I knew their romanticism with tragedy would linger for a few moments. Life continues that way only.

"Last time I went to Calcutta in a conference, I met him. It was about four years from now. We talked a lot about our college days in the post conference cocktail. He looked shabby. May be he realised that his days were numbered. He did not want to panic me and he did not speak anything suggesting he was ill. But that day he talked a lot about life. 'Life is a "chronic" thing like me, Prabhat,' he said. The Lord of the Universe is chronically addicted to life. He keeps on recycling it in some form of other. The Holy Gita says; *the soul cannot be destroyed by weapons, it cannot be blown up by wind, neither can it be decimated by water or fire.* So you see! The soul also remains "chronic." Then what is the harm in my being "chronic"? I have, in fact enjoyed being so.' I had, no notion whatsoever that he would leave us that soon."

"What happened to his family?" asked Ruchi.

"Deepti, his daughter, was in standard nine that time. They stayed in the same Phoolbagan area. I could not visit his house. Until that day, no reconciliation had taken place with his parent. As of today, I hardly have any idea about his wife and daughter. But I wish I knew." I concluded.

"Now let's go for dinner." I wanted to divert the sombre mood in the air.

Rajni left to serve dinner. As she turned back, I could not help notice that her fingers wiping her eyes with a brisk movement.

ELOCUTION

"Discuss throw: first; Arun Dutta, Shastri House. Second; Bikash Banerjee, Subhash House. Third; Pankaj Sarkar, also of Shastri House." The voice of Arati Madam echoed in the air. There was a huge round of applause from the Shastri House tent as the boys stood proudly on the victory stand. This was the annual sports day of the Sector 18 Bengali Medium Lower Secondary School at Rourkela. To make the occasion enjoyable, it was a perfect winter morning. This school is only one of its kind in the city. To make the point clear, Rourkela is in the state of Orissa and most of the schools are run by the Rourkela steel plant, the running force behind the town. Initially, all the lower secondary schools (the schools running classes up to 7th standard) belonged either to Oriya or to Hindi medium. And there was an English medium school as well. It was after intense lobbying of a sizable Bengali speaking population over there the steel plant management had agreed to open this school which had started about ten years' back. The medium of study and all the activities of the school are in Bengali and the diehard lovers of the language have opted to get their wards in the school so that their children do not go wayward from their root in an alien state.

The annual sports day is a big event. There was a large crowd comprising of the students, the parents and some onlookers. The sports ground was buzzing with activity. The teachers were performing various tasks allotted by the headmistress Mrs. Barnali Majumdar, MA, B Ed. She has got a reputation of being a good teacher as well as a strict administrator. Under her guidance the school has earned a good reputation as well. The students were divided into four houses named after four prominent personalities of India: Mahatma Gandhi, Subhash Bose, Jawaharlal Nehru and Lalbahadur Shastri. The students were allotted different tents for the houses with their respective flags implanted in front of the house tents. They also fashioned the badges of the colour of their houses and were generally a happy lot. Boys and girls proficient in sporting activities were having a field day. Some were good enough to get five to six cups on that day. Metallic cups of different sizes are generally given to the winners of the sports event.

Debajyoti wished he could get one of these cups. It was such a nice trophy to flaunt. But being non-athletically built he had always shied away from sports. He was afraid of being rebuked if he tried in track and field events. He looked at the boys and girls running and jumping in the events and sighed. It seemed they were persons from some other planet. He was sick of getting a book as a prize every year. That was given for academic excellence. Debajyoti generally topped in the class. But he did not like the cocoon of academic brilliance. A book as a prize is good, but that does not match aura and glitter of the cups earned by the sports personnel.

"So, what does the first-boy think of Subhash House? Shall we be able to make up from this position?" Subhashis asked Debajyoti from behind. They were all sitting in the common mat in their house.

Debajyoti hated the tag of 'first-boy.' It sounded like an abuse to him; especially on the sports day. It could easily have been translated into: *that is the only thing you are capable of; the dumb studies.* However, he had to look cheerful. "Yes, we still have Bishwanath and Alpana in our house and their events are due."

"Debajyoti-dada, in the prize distribution ceremony you will receive the prize for securing first position in class this year as well. How do you manage to top every year? The Headmistress speaks so highly of you." Arnab Pal of class four quipped. There was genuine tone of respect in his voice. Debajyoti was in 6th standard and it was a ritual in the school to call the senior boys with the suffix 'dada' or elder brother.

Under normal circumstances Debajyoti would have enjoyed a compliment like that. But today he was not in the mood. Yet he smiled politely.

"Mugging is the key word my dear. The longer you spend with those horrific subjects like history, geography etc, the better student you are." Pradeep Roy of class seven made a passing statement to the entertainment of most of them present. But Arnab Roy was a serious student. He did not laugh. "But what about maths? You can't mug that subject," he asked instead. Pradeep remained unperturbed. "Well, you need a little bit of brain as well." He tapped his temple. There was a roar of laughter. Debajyoti's darkish face took a purple hue.

"Studying needs talent and you must give credit to Debajyoti for doing consistently well in the class. You people are jealous of him because you could never match his talent," intruded Monisha, Debajyoti's classmate, "you guys can applaud the sports persons but you can't appreciate his talent! Shame on you." Her beautiful face reddened with anger. Monisha was a genuinely good creature and fought for justice.

Above all she was popular in the entire school. She ranked among the first five in the class and was very good in drama, dancing and recitation of poetry. She had also participated in the inter-state school dance meet few months' back.

However, the argument got buried under a huge roar when Ramakanta Banerjee and Nikhil Naskar of Subhash House completed first in the three-legged race competition. This was unexpected. Few more points were added to the Subhash House. Debajyoti wished the events continued unabated so that he would be left out of the discussion. But that was not to be. The lunch break was announced. The students were given lunch packets; in effect which were snacks packets only. But the children were happy.

The break did not augur that badly for Debajyoti. Dibyendu came to join him for lunch. Dibyendu Paul was a good sportsman. He already had three cups in his kitty. He was good as a person as well.

"Have you ever tried some sports?" Dibyendu asked Debajyoti. "I'm sure you will do well if you give it a sincere try."

"Not much beyond a little bit of football and cricket as per the season in our locality. I am bad in those as well. They are afraid to include me in any team." Debajyoti gave a wry smile.

"That's nothing. It was the same with me before. That made me try harder. It is like studies only. The more you practise and the more you take interest, the better you are." Dibyendu was always encouraging in his attitude. "Meanwhile, don't take those guys seriously. They are simply jealous of you. You will do something great one day."

That cleared the cloud from Debajyoti's mind. That is the charm with childhood. No amount of botheration makes a permanent imprint on the mind. He started to think of positive things. He had a plan made for today. He would take part in the 'go-as-you-like' event. It is during the closing ceremony. It does not require any physical endurance either. The event is more popularly known as 'fancy dress' here. He was carrying his items in a side bag. It was a simple get up he was going to adopt. The chances of winning are remote given the high standard of the competition; but joining there with others is gratifying in itself.

There were the other events which started after lunch. Subhash House finally could not make it to the top. They were edged out by Shastri House. Yet, a close second was not that bad either. They cheered for their respective houses.

"The participants for the fancy-dress competition are to get ready quickly. They are to move to the main hall of school to get themselves prepared." Ghosh Sir's voice was loud and clear in the air. Debajyoti got up and advanced towards the school building.

"Hey, you didn't tell you are participating!" The surprised voice of Subhashis followed him.

"It is nothing much to tell about." Debajyoti brushed aside Subhashis and carried on towards the school building.

Debajyoti's plan was simple. He had borrowed a *lungi* and short *kurta* from his father which needed a little alteration which was done by his mother. A fez cap was also prepared from the extra clothes in his mother's stock. His mother stitches all their clothing; thereby saving money to run a poor household. Debajyoti tied the *lungi* over his shorts and slipped the *Kurta* over the shirt. Then he put on the fez cap and painted his hair popping out of the cap with toothpaste diluted in water. A wad of cotton wool was fixed on the chin with spirit gum to create a goat-beard and a thin ribbon out of the same material was fixed on the upper lip to suffice as a moustache. Then he brought out an old metal frame of a spectacle from the bag and put it on his nasal bridge. Debajyoti had a look at himself in the small mirror he was carrying. His get up was that of an elderly Muslim tailor. He nodded satisfactorily and as a final touch hung a measuring tape on his neck. He rehearsed his dialogues two times. They were simple. These were to the effect that he was an expert tailor from Lucknow and that everyone around was lucky to have him so that they can put up their orders for making dress materials. Then he looked at the other competitors. Shefali Dhar of 7th standard looked grand in her get up of Lord Shiva. Then there was Nripen Roychowdhury; he had dressed as a king. There were others dressed as postman, beggar, vegetable vendor and so on. *I don't stand a chance*, he said to himself, *but I'll give my best under the circumstances.*

And he did his best. The bending of his back to *salaam* the audience, his address to the audience in Urdu; albeit mixed with an accent of Bengali, his movements all went well with the audience. Even he saw a mild nod of appreciation from the headmistress. While returning back to the tent, a plump lady, possibly the mother of a student shouted: "Tailor master, come to my house. I will put up an order." Debajyoti wished his parents were there to enjoy the show. But they have got his father's bicycle only as a mode of conveyance and from that far off it was not feasible for the two to come here. Any hired mode of conveyance would cost dear to his father's pocket. Yet, if only he could get a prize in this event that will double the pleasure of his mother. But then, the others had done equally well too.

Back in the tent, even Subhojit and Pradeep, his perpetual antagonists had a word or two in his praise.

"You are good at acting. And the attire looked so natural on you. I never thought you will do so well in your first shot at this," Subhojit said.

"But Shefali and Nripen were good as well. They are going to give you a run for money. And I must admit they looked great. So, keep your fingers crossed pal." Pradeep looked cheerful.

The prize distribution started. The announcement was being done by Ghosh Sir and Arati Madam in turns. The Additional District Magistrate, the chief guest of the evening was handing over the prizes. First, the prizes for academics were given away. Debajyoti got a book wrapped in printed paper for securing highest marks in class five. He received it without much enthusiasm. It was a routine affair. He sat back amongst few back patting. Then came the day's sports prizes. There was thunderous applause for the sports persons as they reached the podium. Students like Arun Dutta, Dibyendu Paul and Alpana Chakraborty kept coming to the podium and the chief guest got familiar to their names as well. The House Trophies were to be given at the end.

"Now, the prize for fancy dress competition." Arati Madam announced. Debajyoti stood straight. "All the competitors did a great job; but the first prize goes to the boy who did it excellently with the simplest of available material; Debajyoti Mukherjee." There was a mixed reaction from the crowd. Some cheered and some booed. This happens every time while prizes for fancy dress is announced. Debajyoti walked slowly to the podium to receive his prize. Nripen and Shefali got the second and third prizes respectively. Back in the tent most of students congratulated him. But there were also talks like, "Shefali did the best. She was ignored." Debajyoti knew the voice. It was from Jharna Banerjee, one of the closest mates of Shefali. He did not mind. He was happy that there was one more prize to show at home this time. This one was not a cup though; something wrapped in glossy paper. Yet, it did not matter.

The prize distribution was coming to an end. Debajyoti was not listening to the announcements seriously. He did not have anything else to get.

"Hey, Debajyoti! They are calling your name." Monisha poked him from side.

It was true. Ghosh Sir was calling his name alright. He stood first in something else as well! He did not know what it was for. Nevertheless, he made a slow run to receive the prize. The chief guest gave the prize with the words, "Well done boy." He returned confused. He looked at the wrapped box in his hand and shook it. It sounded like a set of crayons. There was a level on the box with the words *FIRST PRIZE: ELOCUTION CONTEST.* He tried to remember hard. *What does 'elocution' mean?* Nothing came. He was not familiar with the ward. He was generally considered good in English language and secured good marks in the subject. But he did not hear anything like that. Monisha asked what the prize was about. He could not give a satisfactory reply. "It was some competition held earlier. I will tell you later," was all he could tell. To his rescue, the House Trophies were being given that time and all the queries got undermined in that rapturous cheer.

While departing for home, Debajyoti thought for once that he would ask Geeta Madam, their English language teacher the meaning of 'elocution,' but a gush of shame refrained him from doing so. *It is going to be ridiculous if I ask the meaning of something I stood first in! I will be a laughing stock to them.*

It was five in the afternoon. Debajyoti started walking towards home. The walk takes about one hour from the school. His house is at sector 4. Due to financial constraints he had not opted for the school bus. He was accompanied by Deepak, Arun and Anup. They were his usual company. Deepak and Arun were brothers and stayed at sector 4 and Anup belonged to the nearby sector 5. Generally they walk at a brisk pace so as to save some time for a game of football or cricket. But they were late as such and there was no chance of a game that day. So they preferred to have a leisurely walk.

"Don't you think the decision to give you the first prize in fancy dress was biased?" Deepak started pestering Debajyoti. "Shefali and Nripen dressed much better. They were hardly being recognised."

"It was the decision of the panel of judges. I did not tell them to give me the prize." Debajyoti countered.

"Whatever you say Deepak, there is a lot of looking-at-the-face thing in our school. If they like someone's face every prize will be given to him. My mother also says so," commented Anup, who failed last year to join these three in class six.

Debajyoti was wondering whether there was something special in his face. But he had seen it in mirror. It looked very plain to him. Even Anup looked much better.

"Why you guys are bothered? You did not get any prize and he got three of them. That's the end of it." Arun came to the help of Debajyoti.

"I even doubt whether he is that good at studies as well. In my opinion, Rekha Samaddar is a better student. Only because Debajyoti has got a reputation as a good student he gets the favour from the teachers while it comes to giving the marks in the annual examinations." The tone of Deepak was vitriolic. There are people, even as children who see the darker side of any glory, but they won't try enough to uplift themselves. "I think Anup is right. There is a looking-at-the-face business."

"Then your face is the worst rated as far as the liking of the teachers is concerned. You barely passed in all the subjects." Arun made a face at his elder brother. Debajyoti and Anup laughed aloud. Arun was average in all the activities but was a happy go lucky boy. *How diverse characters the two brothers have!* Debajyoti wondered.

"But what was the prize you went to receive the third time?" Anup still preferred to linger to the topic of Debajyoti.

This was the thing Debajyoti apprehended. He knew that he would not be able to explain that. "I really don't know." He told truthfully.

"Okay, don't be cross with us. Just show me what it is." Anup was not one to be deterred when he clung to a topic. Debajyoti silently handed over the packet to him.

"Well, let us see," Anup and Deepak halted to have a closer look at the packet. "It says: first prize for elocution. When was this elocution thing done?" Deepak asked.

"I could have told you if I knew the meaning of 'elocution.' I really don't know the meaning of the word." Debajyoti said earnestly.

"Now look at it," Deepak told triumphantly, "our topper does not know the meaning of the word he has got a first prize for. That shows that either nothing like that exists or his knowledge is not good enough."

"Quite possible," Anup added. "My guess is, there was one prize left back and the teachers thought that they should hand the same to their blue eyed boy in the name of some phoney contest.

Debajyoti walked on as if he had committed a crime of late. He tried to think whether anybody else got prize in the same event; but he could not remember that either.

The boys had reached to a point from where Deepak and Arun were to enter their house and Anup and Debajyoti were to make diversions into different directions. "Whatever the contest was, it was Debajyoti's prize all the same. Anup, give it back to Debajyoti," Arun said before entering home. Anup handed it over to its owner and departed.

Human emotions, especially in childhood, are difficult to explain. Debajyoti, who was so elated to get three prizes about an hour back, was remorseful in his thought. He really could not make out why he was given that 'elocution' prize. He tried to recollect whether he did anything worth in recent past. There was no such activity. *Could it be that there is some truth in what Anup and Deepak told? Yes, the teachers like me; but I thought this is because I am good at studies. But is it possible that they have given me the last one for nothing? That sounds absurd. Then there has to be something in which I excelled. I am unable to remember that either. My parents and my younger sister will also ask what the prize is for. What will I answer them?* Debajyoti's house was only five minute's walk from Deepak's house. He was almost there. But his dilemma did not end. At the last turn before his house he had made his decision. *There is no point in carrying a prize home when I don't know what it is for. It may or may not be genuine; but why carry something which is a source of embarrassment to me? No, I can't explain it.* He stopped over the bridge of a large drain adjacent to his house. Then he took out the box containing presumably a crayon set, had a final look at it and finally threw the same in the drain. It floated in the running water. *Good riddance,* he thought.

It was almost dark as Debajyoti entered his house. All the members were present in the house. "I am glad that you got the first prize in fancy dress competition," his father told, "it is always good to participate in other activities along with academics. It helps in the all-round improvement of a student. I wish you to take part in sports in the forthcoming year."

"What did you tell in front of the audience as a tailor master, dada?" Asked the little sister, who was in class four.

Debajyoti smiled and enacted an encore of what he did in the school. She applauded.

"It was all my idea," chirped his mother, "it was plain and simple but effective. Did the kurta fit you alright?" She was basking in her son's glory. "But wash yourself properly first and have some food. You look tired. These discussions can continue later on as well."

It was not before nine at night Debajyoti could find himself alone. There was discussion on various topics like what were the sporting events, who all excelled in sports, what were the other characters in fancy dress, what were the reactions of the teachers and so on. His father recollected the reminiscences of his own school life. The evening was a merry family get together. But during all these things there was something that kept pinching Debajyoti from inside.

As soon as he had the opportunity, he caught hold of the Oxford Dictionary. A, b, c-d, and then there was E, and then e-l-o-, yes it was there! Elocution! The meaning of 'elocution' was: the skill of clear and expressive speech. Origin; Latin. *So, it was a speech competition!* Yes, now Debajyoti remembered vividly; there was indeed a speech competition on the topic 'Village or city; which is a better place to live?' held at the school about three months' back the result of which was never announced. That's why he forgot the event. Moreover, in their school they are more familiar with the term 'debate competition' for such events even if there is no cross arguments on the points made. 'Oration' is another terminology Debajyoti still understood in this matter. But 'elocution'? It was completely out of the world and it went tangentially over his box. He smiled to himself. At least now he was ready face an inquisitive crowd in the school tomorrow. And it was a genuine credit he had earned. After all, it was not a looking-into-the-face thing!

Debajyoti ate his dinner heartily and slept peacefully that night.

------◈------

RIGHT TO IMPORTANCE

"You and your reality shows!" Dr. Pritam Joshi whined while unlacing his shoes sitting on the couch of the dressing room.

"There are many forms of entertainment which do not suit your intellectually greater sense of perception. That does not stop these being popular. At least the TRP ratings do not point to that." Ranjana replied without looking at her husband. She did not like to be disturbed during her favourite TV programmes.

TV watching had been a point of controversy in the Joshi household since long. Pritam Joshi hardly has time to see a TV programme considering his hectic schedule. He works as an orthopaedic surgeon in the Surajpur District Hospital in the state of Chhattisgarh. Whatever time he gets to spend at home, a large chunk of it is occupied in seeing the patients who keeps trickling down there as well. That is why he has to run a well-equipped clinic at his quarter. He is the only orthopaedic surgeon in the vicinity and has a good reputation as well. He works with honesty and integrity. The welfare of patient comes first to him irrespective of his socio economic strata. It is only after 9.00 PM that he has time to relax and that is the time he watches his TV programmes where his choice hovers between news broadcast or an occasional sports telecast. He does not like to be disturbed during this period. That is why there are two television sets in the house. The larger one in drawing room and the portable set in the bedroom. This is also the prime time for family serials and reality shows of which Ranjana is an avid viewer. The two of them remain engaged in their own TV watching pursuits in different rooms during late in the evening and yet there are times when their paths cross and they don't let it go without a dig passed at each other. TV viewing has become easier these days since Diya and Riya, their daughters are away in larger cities pursuing their higher studies. When they are around, they have their choice of programme as well; it used to be the cartoon channels when they were children and the Hindi movies as they grew up. At their mid fifties Pritam Joshi is of the opinion that a bit of poke at each other occasionally might add a little salt to their quiet conjugal life.

"Look at that girl Nikita; isn't she cute? She is playing so fluently as well! Very smart of her; I'm sure she will be the final winner." Ranjana sounded excited. She had forgotten that her husband did not enjoy these shows.

Pritam looked at the ongoing program. It was some stupid game show in which the participants were to answer silly questions while playing some easy games. Nikita, the girl in question was pretty indeed and was very excited about the goings on. The camera was focused on her parents whose faces were inflated with joy giving the impression as if their daughter had reached the top of Mt. Everest. Pritam felt sad for the girl. The girl would feel on cloud nine for a few days and be congratulated by all and sundry known to her and then fade into oblivion for good. If only she could learn something creative, she could have savoured her glory for longer period. Pity that they hanker for this type of flashes rather than developing skills of sustaining nature.

"What is the use of such short moments of glory which people are bound to forget very soon? Even you, you will forget her name tomorrow." Pritam said bitterly.

"You and your cynicism! Can't you see anything straight?" Ranjana reacted, "Can everyone be a Manmohan Singh, Shahrukh Khan or a MS Dhoni?" Then added with fervor, "And may be a Dr. Joshi for that matter. But everyone has got a right to enjoy his or her moment of glory; however short it may be. It can be a treasure for the girl to keep a lifetime. Well, tell me frankly, don't you enjoy the moments when the patients fold their hands in gratitude to you? Or when you are called as a guest of honour in some public function?"

Pritam reflected on that. He had to agree that the statement was true; at least partially. He felt happy when a patient expressed his or her gratitude when he or she returned to their daily routine after long periods of disability. He thought that was a doctor's best incentive to carry on. As far as being a guest of honour was concerned, he felt honoured all right but did not like it to drag long. He prayed for the function to end as soon as possible.

Ranjana realised that she had proven a point. She smiled broadly. "Why search far off? Look at our own Ganpatpal. Doesn't he relish his moments of importance?"

It was true. Ganpatpal did enjoy whatever attention he received. That must be a basic human nature. Pritam Joshi started pondering over Ganpatpal.

It was about three years' back. Diya and Riya were both at home that time. Pritam had just finished seeing patients in his evening clinic. Ranjana approached Pritam with a man at her toes. The man was short; may be a shade over five, thinly built with a prominent head conspicuous by a huge bald lined with a strip of grey and black hair and a diminutive smile.

"He is our Punia's husband. He is in search for a job." Ranjana informed as if she had come to an employment exchange. Punia was the housemaid of the Joshi household. Ranjana believed in obliging housemaids on some plea or other which she thought ensured better service from them.

"I can't generate jobs. I'm a doctor; not a businessman." Pritam announced bluntly.

"You can still help the poor guy. Isn't the assistant of your clinic absconding since a fortnight or so? There is little possibility that he will turn up at all. When you are around, this fellow can help you out. In other times he can help in gardening as well as do the errands of the household which are aplenty." Ranjana was highly optimistic about placing him somewhere. Knowing his wife, Pritam knew well that possibly he had already been assured of the job by Ranjana. There was no point in dragging the thing far.

"What's your name?" asked Pritam.

"Ganpat." The man smiled. It showed a lack of self-confidence as he scratched his baldhead. The man should be his own age. He had an unshaven face.

"How did you manage your livelihood so long?" Pritam asked the pertinent question.

"I used to work as a contractual labourer with one of the builders. I had to be out of job for a month as I broke my hand. You only treated me then Sahib." Ganpat showed his right forearm. It looked fine to Pritam.

"Your hand looks alright to me. Why don't you resume your job?"

"They have kept another man in my place." Ganpat scratched his head again.

Dr. Joshi felt for the man. These builders make loads of money at the expense of their labourer and yet when it comes to their welfare there seems to be none existent.

"How much did you earn there?" He asked.

"Rs. 100 a day. But the payment was not regular. He paid as per his convenience; often there was a delay in paying us." Ganpat confessed with honesty.

"Alright, you can start from tomorrow. You will be paid the same amount as you used to get there. And to the best of my ability I'll try to pay you in time; but in return I want full devotion from your side. If I don't see your work satisfactory, your job will be terminated immediately. Did I make my point clear?"

"Yes Sahib, I assure you that I'll not give you an opportunity to complain." Ganpat smiled again, this time with a little more of confidence.

So Ganpat stayed. He did not give an opportunity to complain and, he seemed to love his job. But there were some jobs which were his favourites; like helping the doctor in the clinic, the tit-bits of which he learned with élan; then there was the cleaning of Pritam's car which did not warrant a reminder and the gardening job. As far as the household errands were concerned, he did these with a bit of grumbling. Partly this was because of the constant bossing around of Ranjana over him. Ranjana took him to be a personal property of sorts and he did not seem to like it. He would prefer a job assigned to him to be completed in his own way in the best possible manner. Independence was the key word for him. Being supervised in between took the charm out of it. Yet it was a minor problem considering the fact that Ranjana kept good care of Ganpat as well. She would keep any delicacy made at house for her Ganpat Bhayia; his dress would be taken care of; mostly from the used lot of Pritam, with an occasional new dress as well. So Ganpat spent his time with a reasonable degree of contentment.

One morning a young lad knocked at the door of Dr. Joshi. Dr. Joshi answered the bell himself.

"What do you want young man?" Pritam Joshi thought that he had come with a medical problem, as is often the case.

"I'm Chhotu, my father works here. He has sent a gourd for you. We cultivate it at our house." He showed a fresh gourd to Pritam.

"Who is your father?"

"He is Ganpatpal Sonwane."

That was the day Pritam realised that Ganpat had such a heavy sounding official name as well. He was so fascinated by the name that he started calling Ganpat by the name of Ganpatpal or Sonwane-Ji when in best of mood, amounting to blushing and more vigorous bald scratching from the man concerned. But Pritam liked Ganpat all the same. Overall, he fitted into the household nicely. He had his own style of addressing though; and sometime an unusual accent, which took time to be understood. Pritam and Ranjana were *uncle* and *aunty* to him that was objected by some outsiders considering the fact that he was nearly the same age as the couple; but he did not relent. In his opinion, this was the best way to show his respect to them. Joshi couple of course had no objection to it. Diya and Riya were *Badi-didi* and *Chhoti-didi* respectively. These two girls also liked their Ganpat Bhayia (yes, Bhayia to them as well; like that of their mother) in spite of the fact that they shared some good humor at his expense.

Once Riya approached Pritam with a wicked smile on her face. "Dad, whatever hair Ganpat Bhayia is left with is receding fast."

"Why?" Pritam asked.

"It's because of Mom. He is afraid that he might be called any moment by her and a fault would be found with him. No amount of delicacies offered to him is going him to get rid of his fear psychosis."

Pritam laughed aloud.

"And that is not the end of his plight," Riya said.

"Is there something more?" Pritam was suspicious that the arrow might be directed to him. His daughters were capable of everything.

"The other day Ganpat Bhayia was cleaning a scissor in the clinic. His wife Punia Didi called, 'are you listening?' and can you guess what happened?"

"What?"

"The scissor fell from his hand and to his embarrassment, I and didi were standing in front of him?"

"What did he do then?" Pritam sounded amused.

"He simply picked up the scissor from ground, gave his classic smile and said to us, 'my wife,' and finished with a unique 'heh__heh'." This 'heh__heh' was a unique sound Ganpat emitted whenever he tried to convert his smile into a laugh.

On another occasion both the girls came to Pritam shouting slogans of "Long live Ganpatpal."

An astonished Pritam asked, "What's that new prank about?"

"Ganpat Bhayia has done an act of bravery. He deserves a bravery award." Diya said.

"What for?"

"For the first time in his life he dared to answer Mom on her face. On Mom's repeated calls for some job he kept quiet for some time and finally appeared before her to say, 'why do you keep shouting when I'm so nearby? The job will be done; but let me finish the previous one first.'"

"Didn't your Mom react?"

"She kept quiet for a change."

Ganpatpal had been like that. He was afraid of his *aunty,* he was afraid of his wife; he did not speak much in front of Dr. Joshi possibly out of fear; or may be respect. Yet he had an independent soul of his own. This was evident once Pritam asked him to come early in the morning.

"I'll come in the morning; but I can't make it before 9.00 AM." Ganpat scratched his bald.

"What important job do you have in the morning?" Pritam was sarcastic.

"I'll have to sell *bareth.*"

"What the hell this *bareth* is?"

Ganpat fumbled and did not say a thing. Ranjana, who stood nearby burst out giggling. That was the time Pritam learnt that *bareth* was Ganpat's version of bread. He used to sell bakery made bread and biscuit from door to door in his bi-cycle every morning.

"I didn't know that so long!" Pritam complained when they two were alone.

"Because you never asked him," Ranjana smiled.

"Did you ask him?"

"No, I didn't have to. He loves to talk. And when he talks I listen to him carefully. He is too scared of you to talk I believe."

"How much does he earn selling his *bareth*?" Pritam smiled too.

"Very little, as far as I know."

"Then why does he do it?" Pritam was puzzled.

"This is a million dollar question," Ranjana relaxed on the bed over a cushion, "tell me, what's your best mode of relaxation?"

Pritam considered it for a moment. "I think keeping quiet for sometime in the day when I like to be left to myself; may be taking an occasional drink during that period."

"Exactly," Ranjana sounded as if she had made a point, "you like to keep to yourself as you have to deal with so many persons a day. It is just the other way round with Ganpat. He has to keep quiet and subdued, for that matter, almost all the day. Be it here or at his house."

"Subdued at his house?" Pritam exclaimed.

"Yes, he is the person who takes orders and the others speak it out; be it his wife or his children."

"You seem to have gathered a lot of facts about Ganpat." Pritam smiled.

"Don't forget that I'm a female; it's our natural instinct. Moreover, Ganpat loves to talk, given a chance. Then two and two makes four only."

"We were talking about selling bread," reminded Pritam.

"Yes, that's his leeway to freedom, to live like a man. I've seen him selling bread. He looks a different man altogether. He travels from door to door, talks to people on equal footing; on a wide range of subjects ranging from increasing cost of vegetables to the marriage of someone's daughter and to various social issues. There are people like elderly parents of the house or infirm persons who await his arrival so that they can have their share of discussion as well. Then there are the stray dogs. Some of them are his favourites. He throws them a piece of bread and biscuit on his way. He gets his due regard from them with the wagging of their tails. He can't leave this *bareth* selling of his. It is an addiction with him. The breads not consumed are used at his house."

"Why don't you start writing 'bout human nature? You are such an avid observer of it!" Pritam marvelled.

Ranjana tried to ignore the dig if there was one. "No sir, I'm quite happy watching my TV serials. By the way, have you seen Ganpat ever selling his bread? I also purchase bread from him often."

"Never. I even didn't know he is in this business." Pritam confessed.

"Very much like you," commented his wife. "He dresses well, hums some movie song and most often there is a betel leaf wrapped in tobacco in his mouth during these sojourns;" Ranjana laughed, "I love to see him during this act of his."

Pritam was fascinated by this tale. He realised that every man has got a right to his importance. It is something like right to work, right to education or right to information the Govt. is passing from time to time. He started observing Ganpat more closely. One evening, while entering his clinic he heard Ganpat talking to a patient's relative.

"The hand of your child is broken. Doctor Sahib is going to plaster it. You must not allow the child to get it wet. That hampers in bone healing." Ganpat was advising.

"You seem to know a lot about these things. You must have worked for a long time with him." The villager seemed impressed.

"Not a long time really; it is only a couple of years. But I work hard and that's why I learn fast; heh____heh." Ganpat never let an opportunity go when it came to impress someone.

"Are you solely employed to assist the doctor?" The man was indeed impressed.

"Not really; it is only a part of my job. In addition, I've to do some household work, look after the garden and so on. The job is tough all right; but doctor uncle and aunty realise the same and they have increased my daily wage to Rs. 120 a day from Rs. 100 a day without my asking for it. They are good people. That's why I got stuck here. Otherwise I have my *bareth* selling business; if I devote full time in that, I can earn a decent living as well."

It was at this point Pritam made his entry into the clinic. The conversation stopped and he was engaged with the patients. When the clinic was empty, he started talking to Ganpat.

"I would appreciate if you don't advise the patients in my absence."

"I thought it will help you. I was only trying to help." Ganpat lowered his head and gave it its customary scratch.

"And I thought it was *my* job to advise the patient." Pritam told.

"It will not be repeated, uncle." Ganpat left.

One morning Ganpat came to Pritam and scratched his head. "I want a leave for today."

"Is there anything important?" Pritam asked.

"Well,___sort of. My elder son is getting married."

Pritam had no idea of the family background of Ganpat. "How many children do you have? Only one son of yours I've seen. He didn't seem to be of marriageable age to me."

"That was Chhotu. He reads in college. My daughter is already married. It's Pyarelal, the elder son that is getting married." Ganpat announced, a shade remorsefully though.

"You don't look happy about it. Won't you invite us for the same?"

"I'd have loved to. But it is not a regular kind of marriage," and before Pritam could ask anything more Ganpat left; adding, "aunty knows everything about it."

That night Pritam asked Ranjana about the marriage of this son.

"This Pyarelal works in a private factory at Ambikapur (about 40 km. from Surajpur) and earns about Rs. 5000 per month. He does not come to his parents' house and spends all his money on the family of a girl with whom he is alleged to be in love. Now they are getting married at Ambikapur. He had told Ganpat and Punia yesterday only that they might attend the function if they liked. And also that it did not matter if they plan to give it a skip." Ranjana was almost fuming. "It's better to have no son than having a son like this," she added as a corollary.

There is no dearth of such incidence, thought Pritam. "Now I realise why importance is so important to Ganpat," he sighed. "I wonder what sort of position he will be in at the marriage function!"

"Yet it is *their* son. What can they do?" Ranjana felt for the couple.

Over further conversation that night, Pritam gathered some more domestic facts of Ganpatpal Sonwane. At the constant bickering of Punia the couple went to their Bihar village once where they had some ancestral land. It was their portion they wanted to sell off so that they could have some ready cash at hand. By that time, Ganpat's brothers had taken hold of the land bribing the police over there. Punia was in favor of going for a legal action. But Ganpat thought it beyond his dignity to draw his brothers to the court. Possibly he was aware of the futility of the process as well. They were literally shown the door there by his brothers.

Then there was the case of their daughter. She was married in a family that constantly tortured the girl. When Ganpat and Punia talked to her in laws, they demanded money in lieu of a decent up keeping of their daughter-in-law. The *Panchayat* of the village finally asked Ganpat and Punia to take their daughter back with them; that too under the precarious condition of her advanced pregnancy.

Such ignominy throughout his life! Pritam thought about it. *He deserves every bit of attention and happiness he can gather.* And there were odd occasions when it came though.

Ranjana was preparing *Chhole-Bhature* one morning. The preparation was being made in the honour of the daughters who had come home on some holiday. The *Bhature* part of it required a special mashing of wheat and flour. That job was allotted to Ganpat with the words that all the three ladies of the house wanted to learn the process from him. The fact was, he is supposed to be good at that. These are the things that elated Ganpat. Later on, when he was washing Pritam's car, he told Pritam: "Uncle, may be the cleaning will not be that great today as my hands are feeling a bit tight."

"Any particular reason?" Pritam could guess that it was just a prelude.

"Aunty and the didis wanted to learn the mashing of *Bhature* from me. It had to be mashed tight for a long period. I learnt it the hard way when I was working for a *dhaba* (roadside restaurant) few years back. The *dhaba* owner was very fond of me and never wanted that I_____"

It was another bout of self-praising of Ganpat and Pritam left quietly nodding his head and concealing a smile.

The big occasion came for Ganpat one day. It was about six months' back. Ganpat was heading towards his home at about 8.30 in the evening. It was raining heavily and he walked towards his house holding an umbrella in one hand and his bicycle in the other. As such, it was not possible to ride his cycle even on the tar-laden roads; it was more difficult when he neared his house. The road was a slender mud-built one with a variety of bushes and weeds lining it. To compound his misery, there was no electricity in their area. Sparse light from the kerosene oil lamps made an eerie play of light and shade. Ganpat stepped carefully. There was lightning and thunder from the sky in addition to rain. Nevertheless, he was more concerned about snakes than any other thing. It happened then. There was a pandemonium from a distance. It was of a hostile nature. The sound was closing in. Ganpat got scared and started walking fast on the slippery path. He thought he might topple. However, he did not topple; but someone else did. The man was running in his direction fast. As he approached the shadow like figure of Ganpat, he stopped for a split second and then started afresh. It was then he slipped in the mud and stumbled. He got into a tangle with Ganpat's bicycle and open umbrella and fell on the ground. Ganpat could not keep his balance and fell on the entire heap thus made. The man cried in pain. "I think I've broken my leg. Why don't you lift the hell of your body from me?" Ganpat tried to oblige but slipped and fell back again. While attempting a third such manoeuvre he saw that a group of people had encircled the two of them. "Here is the thief!" One amongst them shouted. The others echoed in unison. They lifted a puzzled Ganpat out of the mess and then pulled out the man from underneath the bicycle. The man was hardly recognisable under the smear of mud on his feature. He limped heavily and cried in pain and fear. He trembled and a bag, which Ganpat did not spot earlier, fell from his hand. One in the mob gathered the bag from the ground and the others started showering blows and kicks on the person. This continued for some time before a middle-aged person with golden-rimmed spectacles and of respectable looks reached the scene of action. Ganpat knew that man. He was Naveen Mittal, the biggest jeweller of the area and a politically powerful person in the local circle.

"Hey, you rogues! You don't have to kill the person and put me into trouble." Mittal shouted and the manhandling came to a standstill. "Pappu, could you recover the loot?"

The tall man, who had taken hold of the bag handed it over to Mr. Mittal. "Yes sir; but it would not have been possible had this brave man not nabbed the thief and overpowered him." He pointed his finger at Ganpat.

The chain of events had gone too fast for Ganpat to make a decent analysis of the situation. He was exhausted by that time. He smiled nervously at Naveen Mittal and folded his hands. The businessperson was impressed all the same. "It takes courage to overpower a huge person with the small frame of yours." He pulled the right hand of Ganpat with both his hands and shook it vigorously. "You don't realise what you've done. The bag contained ornaments worth more than forty lakh. You have not only saved me the amount; you saved me humiliation as well."

Then he looked at the others: "Just see, what courage can lead to," before turning to Ganpat again, "why you were heading this way?"

"I live in one of those huts," he pointed to the row of huts not far off from there, "it so happened that I was going home and saw this man coming___"

"And you nabbed him. That was a great job done." Mittal completed the sentence for Ganpat. "And what do you do for a living?"

"I sell *bareth* in the morning and do some odd jobs___"

"He is the bread seller sir. I've seen him selling bread and biscuit in the area in morning." One of the men in the group said. "What's your name by the way?"

"Ganpat;" Ganpat said nervously.

Naveen Mittal patted Ganpat on his shoulder. "I know how to honor a brave man. You will be felicitated soon." Then he turned to the man called Pappu. "Pappu, have you got your cell phone with you?"

"Yes sir," Pappu replied.

"Take a snap of this Ganpat." Pappu obliged.

All of them left and Ganpat went home. He did not mention anything about this to his family. He had a disturbed sleep as well. He pondered hard over the issue. *It all happened accidentally. A thief was caught. Naveen Mittal was glad about the incidence. But why did they take my photograph? Can there be a catch in this? Rich people have their own tricks. Hope I do not land up in some trouble. And what is this damned 'felicitate' thing? I'll ask doctor uncle tomorrow.*

Dr. Pritam joshi was getting ready for the hospital in the morning. Ganpat came near him and scratched his head. Pritam did not notice it and sat on the breakfast table. Ganpat followed him.

"Uncle, I was wondering what might be meant by the term 'felicitate.'" Ganpat smiled more nervously than ever.

"Why, who is felicitating whom?" Pritam told casually.

"Naveen Mittal said that I will be felicitated."

"What did you do so that he will felicitate you?" Pritam was surprised.

"It so happened that, I____"

At that point, Ranjana entered the dining table with a local newspaper in her hand.

"See what our Ganpat Bhaiya has done. His photograph is also there in the paper." She sounded very excited.

Pritam took the paper. This paper is published from nearby Ambikapur. A page is devoted exclusively for news of the district and nearby. There was the photograph of Ganpatpal being cheered by a group of people. The head line went thus: *Rare feat of bravery; humble bread seller saves jewellery worth 40 lakh.* Underneath there was a detailed account of how Ganpat overpowered the thief running away with the jewellery from the shop of renowned jeweller Naveen Mittal.

"So, that's why he wants to felicitate you," said a cheerful Pritam, "felicitating you means he wants to honor you for what you did. But how did you do it exactly?"

Colors had returned to Ganpat. He gave an exact account of what happened last evening. Pritam and Ranjana both laughed aloud.

"Well, there are times when the luck is on your side. However, don't miss the felicitation if there is any. May be he will give you some gift or something." Ranjana told in a serious note.

"Can I keep that page with me, Aunty?" Ganpat asked.

"Of course you can, it is *your* page." Ranjana was happy.

The felicitation was done that evening itself. Naveen Mittal made sure all the dignitaries of the town and reporters were present in the function. Dr. Joshi was also amongst the invitees. It included the collector of the district as well as the local MLA. Ganpat was made to sit beside Mittal on the podium in the same row as the collector and the MLA. The VIPs spoke a lot of good things about Ganpat which was extended to the topic of the need of the hour for people to be honest and courageous. The VIPs used the stage to good effect to enhance their future prospect. Finally, Ganpat was presented with a shawl and a cheque of Rs. 5000. Ganpat was asked to say a few words about the incidence. The poor fellow had had enough of this spotlight and his courage failed. He simply got up, folded his hands to one and all present over there and sat down. However, it was taken as the humility of a poor man and it went well with the occasion. A photograph of Ganpat was taken with the VIPs.

The next evening as Dr. Joshi was about to enter his clinic he saw about fifty people thronging in there and asking Ganpat about his heroics. Ganpat was smiling and was back in his elements. Dr. Joshi delayed his entry deliberately. Instead, he sat on a chair at the adjoining door and listened to Ganpat.

"It so happened that, I saw the man coming from a distance and I had my plan ready. Yes, I was afraid a bit; but should that deter me from stopping a thief? No, I decided to go ahead with my plan. I tangled the legs of the man with the handle of my umbrella. He fell down and I jumped on him. Rest of the story you all know." He brought out two paper cuttings of consecutive days; one in which he was being cheered by a handful of persons and the other in company with the VIPs. "Mittal Sahib knows how to reward a person." The narration ended with the prodigal mixture of laugh and smile, "heh__heh."

THE ENGLISH WAYS

The summer evening at Achintya Kumar Mukherjee's house was vibrant with the animated discussion about FDI or foreign direct investment. The important participants of the discussion were the son, the son-in-law and the nephew of Achintya. His son-in-law was of the opinion that the Americans would pacify the Government of India in getting the bill passed and the other two did not share the view. Also the pros and cons of the impact of the bill on Indian retail market were being discussed over tea and fresh snacks. At eighty-three, Achintya was a mere listener. He had his own views though, but he thought it better to listen rather than speak out. He was in fact enjoying the proximity to his younger relations in his own house. 'Own house!' he rejoiced. It is something he never dreamt of when he had migrated as a refugee at an age of seventeen in the year 1947 from East Pakistan. He came with his family as near pauper. His father, not being of a man of materialistic bend, could not handle his properties which never were substantial in the first place. He had made his journey through the torrid course and finally landed up at a point where there was not much to boast of, yet sufficient to live a respectable living.

Did they say something about the Americans motivating the India Government to accept their ways? Thought Achintya. What is so new about it? The English have always had their ways of getting something done. To Achintya, there is no basic difference between a British and an American. They remain English. There is nothing to assume that Achintya had been a freedom fighter or a nationalist. Far from that. But as a boy in his teens, he was curious enough to attend to the meetings and rallies held around his native district of Khulna in East Pakistan. There was a general consensus amongst the political circle just prior to independence that the Hindu dominated Khulna would be given to India and Murshidabad, having a sizable number of Muslim populations would go to Pakistan. But Lord Mountbatten, the then Viceroy of India, for whatever political consideration, did just the other way round on the eve of declaring independence. He and the English in general, had his ways, thought Achintya. At his ripe old age, Achintya boasted of a good memory complimented by reasonably good physical health. Often he remembered his wonderful journey of struggle in this country and it remained vivid. Then something, pertaining to the ways of the English, yet noting to do with the political or financial scenario of the country came to his mind. It was stored in a fond corner of his memory chamber. He had, in fact narrated the story to his grand children and they had enjoyed it, in their own simple way.

It was 1948, the great Gandhi was assassinated few months' back. Achintya was 18 and he was in his first ever job. Nothing great, but it was interesting all the same. He was the supervisor of labourers of a forest contractor. The contractor was known to one of his relations in Calcutta and that was how he grabbed the job. Being a matriculate, it was easy for him to keep the records as well as look after the day to day works of the labourers. His work place ranged from forest blocks of Barsuan to that of Birmitrapur in the state of Orissa. Headquarter was at Birmitrapur. The contractor, one Biren Dutta was a good natured man. He developed a liking for this homeless boy and offered him a room to stay with his family. Achintya gelled well with the joint family comprising of a lot of children of various denominations. Over a period, he went on to be a part of the family. The children in particular were very fond of Achintya. He shared his experience in the jungle with the children over a refreshing cup of tea in the evening. Achintya had a penchant for storytelling and his descriptions kept the children spell bound. He was having a good time overall.

On that eventful day Achintya was returning from his work back to Birmitrapur. They were to cut the state demarcated trees in a forest zone about 20 kilometres away from Birmitrapur. The forests were denser than it is today. It consisted mostly of *shaal, mahuls* and teak trees. There were myriads of birds which kept chirping and a sizable number of wild animals, mostly fox, bear and elephant. Achintya was in a truck beside the driver and there were about a score of labourers in the back of the truck with their tools. The sun was about to set making an excellent hue of crimson in the western sky. The birds were returning to their nests in flocks. In spite of these being regular events, Achintya was enjoying the sunset through the window of the truck. Suddenly the truck halted with screeching sound of the break. There was a girl of twelve or thirteen who came to a standstill following a run in front of the truck and begged the truck to stop. It was a tribal girl and she was panting and perspiring heavily. On the top of that she was panicky.

"What happened?" asked Achintya agitatedly. "Do you realise you could have got smashed under the truck?" he had picked up the tribal language well as it helped in his work.

The girl was still panting. "Pick me up in your truck Babu, and we can talk later. I have to get off from this place as fast as I can." She looked back at the nearby hill in panic.

"Alright, hop up on the truck and we can do the talking later." Achintya opened the side door for her.

"Let's get out of here fast." She sat on Achintya's side and limped on his shoulder in a slumber. She was exhausted. They drove off from there. After quarter of an hour or so she came back to her senses. She looked around and smiled.

"What happened?" Achintya asked.

"I had a great escape," said the girl exposing her uneven teeth, "it is all because of this," she pointed to her waist. There was a *gamchha* tied on it over her sari. *Gamchha* used to be a common addendum to the dress code of the people of that area. It is a rectangular piece of cotton cloth large enough to wrap around the waist and change one's cloth. It has got multipurpose functions like carrying one's food, wiping of body and face, collect some utility items and tying in the same, taking an occasional bath in the pond and so on. In the girl's case, the gamchha was tied to her waist with tight knots and a portion of it was swollen in a large lump. Achintya did not notice it in the beginning. He noticed the lump carefully. It moved a little.

"What is there?" he was curious.

"I'll show you," she said excitedly. "But will you stop the truck first?"

The driver also seemed as curious as Achintya. He stopped the truck without waiting for an order. The girl untied the knot of the gamchha from her waist and placed it over the seat carefully. Achintya and the driver stooped over to see the content within. As soon as she unfolded the piece of cloth, the driver cried out in excitement, "Goodness gracious! These are tiger cubs!!"

Indeed they were. There were three tiny yellow cubs which looked like kittens but they were unmistakably the cubs of tiger. Achintya had never seen a tiger in that area although he had heard of their existence in remote part of the jungle.

"Where did you find these, girl?" he asked with unabated excitement.

The hitherto fear in the girl was gone. Now she felt like having done something heroic. She narrated her story with an amount of pride. She had gone into a remote part of the forest on the other side of the hill in search of firewood. Her folks were far away with the cattle. That was the time she heard some squeaking at the foot of the hill. It seemed to be one from some young animal. She stepped carefully in that direction and was stunned to find a tiger cub protruding its head out from the cover of fresh leaves in a shallow ditch. She was so panic-stricken that she froze behind a tree. She guessed the mother tigress must be around. Within a minute she spotted the mother though. The tigress was heading in the opposite direction possibly in search of pray. It crossed a canal and headed farther away. Then, in a moment's insanity, the girl ran to the ditch and took up all the cubs, three in total, in her gamchha and tied it in her waist. Then she ran with all her might in the direction opposite to the mother tigress. It struck her later that the mother might follow the scent of her cubs and catch up with her. She ran like mad and thus encountered the truck on the road.

"You must be crazy!" said Achintya as she finished her tale. "What are you going to do with them? You can neither keep them in your village nor can you return them to their mother. Either way you are in trouble. Have you thought what your elders are going to tell when they come to know of it?"

The girl of course had never thought of it. "I have not given it a thought," she confessed. Then she added rather coyly, "I thought maybe I will earn some money from selling the cub."

"Who is going to buy them?" wondered Achintya, "Pawan, will you buy the tiger cubs?" he asked the driver.

Pawan protruded his tongue in embarrassment. "A humble driver like me has got to do nothing with tiger cubs. Please don't embarrass me Babu-Ji."

The commotion in the front seat had brought the curious bunch of labourers to encircle the front of the truck. They marvelled at the sight of the cubs. One of the females even was bold enough to caress one of the cubs.

"Babu, I don't want any money. All I want is to get rid of these cubs and go home." The girl suddenly was on the verge of tear seeing the impending darkness.

Kalua, one of the elderly labourers came up with a solution. "Babu-Ji, why don't you take the cubs with you? You stay in the town where there can be no access of the tigress. Moreover, you have got the necessary infrastructure to keep the cubs with you."

Everyone hailed the idea and there was a general feeling of cheerfulness. The labourers thought that they could have an access to seeing the cubs in future as well. Achintya was a favourite amongst the labourers. But he thought they overestimated him. They thought him something equivalent to the contractor himself. Moreover, Birmitrapur was only an improvised village in the guise of a town. It had a limestone query owned by a private company and that was why some basic amenities were available there.

Achintya thought fast. There was no way he could abandon the cubs. *Let me take them with me and live the rest to Biren Dutta Babu, my boss. Let him decide about the future of the cubs.* He agreed reluctantly. They had to take a detour to reach the village of the girl. She was dropped at the beginning of the village. Achintya searched his pocket. There was a crumbled five rupee note in it. He silently handed over the bank note to the girl. She had had enough for the day. The girl accepted it gleefully and ran away.

While Achintya reached home, that is Biren Dutta's house to be precise, he saw almost all the members of the house to be present there. He was a little late. Without any preamble he called everybody and produced the three tiger cubs from his canvas bag. He kept them on a mat in the floor. There was a cacophony of exclamatory sounds. 'Wow,' 'o my God,' 'hey Ram', 'what have you done' and likewise. Biren Dutta looked at him sternly. Achintya scratched his head and explained the entire situation. Meanwhile, Adharshila Devi, Brien's mother brought a saucer full of cow's milk and offered it to the cubs. The cubs did not show any apathy to cow's milk and slurped it with relish. Two of them even emitted sounds of gratitude towards Adharshila. The sound, however, was nowhere near that of a growling of their own species; it rather resembled the mewing of a cat.

"Let me have a close look at the cubs," declared Naren Babu, the elder brother of Biren. Naren had spent quite a portion of his life in jungle and was a self acclaimed expert on wild life. "Hmm," he declared, "they are hardly a day or two old. Their eyes haven't opened properly yet. Difficult to make them survive. Two are females and this one is a male." He pointed it fingers at one of the cubs on his right.

"Such tiny creatures! Wonder what is going through the mind of their mother!" Nalini Devi, Biren's wife came out with her feminine empathy with a mild chuckle.

For the night the cubs were rested in a cane basket with cushions of old blanket after another saucer full of cow's milk having been fed to them. There was a cynical remark from Biren, "Tigers fed on cow's milk!" However, the others preferred to ignore it.

Post dinner, there was a family meeting in which a general consensus was taken about the fate of the tiger cubs. The young brigade was all for keeping the cubs at home. Ladies did not utter a word. Those days, conservation of wild life laws was not in vogue. Even if there was any, they were not half as stringent as that of present day

"Don't you realise they are tiger cubs, not kitten or puppies!" retorted Biren. "Even if they survive, they are going to grow up into full grown tigers shortly. How can we keep them? Impossible."

"Let them grow up first, and then we can have other thoughts. We can keep them for time being." It was an opinion from Paltu, son of Naren. At an age of fourteen, he was the head of the young brigade. He was supported unanimously by the other children.

"Even if a tiger grows on cow's milk, it will grow up to be a tiger only," advocated Naren. "What if they gobble you up when they grow up?"

"It never does so. If a wild animal is kept as pet, it never harms its keeper. There is a story in our book in which a lion remembered its master years after it departed from him." Paltu said. The younger ones were impressed with the knowledge of their elder brother. Paltu's father, however, remained unimpressed.

"Keep those stories limited to your curriculum only," Naren said, "I doubt anything of that kind happens in real life."

The meeting ended in a deadlock for the night. Biren said he would take the opinion of Mr. Blackwell in the morning. James Blackwell was the General Manager of the Bird Mining Company which did business in limestone. He was generally considered to be a knowledgeable person in the locality.

For next three days the tiger cubs remained at the custody of Biren Dutta's house. The enthusiastic children christened them as Raunak for the male and Varnamala and Sharbari for the females. Even Biren had to agree that the names were in compliance with the royal nature of the animals. The cubs had started waddling and falling around their basket. On the fourth day, the great James Blackwell appeared in person to Biren Dutta's house. He was fascinated to see the tigers. It was a long cherished desire of tall and robust Blackwell to keep a tiger ever since he stepped in India.

"Look Mr. Dutta, it will be difficult on your part to keep the tigers with you as they grow up," he told Biren. "There is a problem with the diet and with the upkeep of the tigers. I can take the help of a veterinarian if I like. Such tiny cubs are difficult to be returned to the forest as well. Moreover, the forest officials might cause a problem or two in this regard, but I can handle it. What I suggest is I keep the cubs till they grow up and then we can hand them over to the forest officials."

If Blackwell thought it would be an easy task to motivate Biren, he was right. But what he did not anticipate was the amount of resistance he was to encounter from the children. They clasped the cubs to their chest and vehemently refused to hand them over to Blackwell. Biren was irate with the children. But Blackwell was a patient and reasonable man. He advised Biren to respect the sentiment of children. Finally, he could convince the children that he would take only one cub with him as he was as passionate as them to have a tiger cub. He also said that the children were free to visit his house whenever they wanted to see the cub. Reluctantly, Sharbari was handed over to Blackwell. Biren was reasonably pleased at the settlement as he wanted to appease Blackwell. He had some business interest with Blackwell.

Days passed by. Sharbari was rechristened Angelina by Blackwell. She was kept under strict supervision of an English vet who made a diet chart for Angelina. On the other hand, Raunak and Varnamala continued on the diet fixed by Adharshila on consultation with Naren. Paltu, Soumen, Riki and other children spent a major part of the day playing with Raunak and Varnamala. They were not afraid of the cubs in the least. The cubs started running and walking in the courtyard of the house. On the negative side, the children spent bare minimum period for studies. In addition, the neighbours came in flocks to see the cubs and issued warnings in advance. 'If we see our poultry or cattle being damaged in future, then be prepared for the consequence,' and things like that. Biren thought that he would put them in cages as they grow up a little more, irrespective of what the children had to say. He discussed the size of the two cages to be made with Achintya.

He did not have to plan for two cages. Raunak died all of a sudden. It was about one month after they were brought. By that time they were on the gradual process of weaning to solid foods like slices of chicken or mutton or boiled eggs. They had grown up to the size of full grown cats by that time and were attacking lizards and cockroaches. The reason of death of Raunak was not clear. Naren attributed it to cow's milk, but he could not explain why Varnamala was not affected by similar diet. Adharshila was of the opinion that it was same as humans; the females survive adversities better than the males.

Varnamala grew up to be three months' old. She adapted to homely conditions with ease. There was a regular supply of mutton from the local butcher for her. She started resembling a young tigress, though not fully grown. She had to be chained as she started being hostile to the goats and poultry. Not that she wanted to kill them for food; it was possibly because of her inherent instincts. Surprisingly, she obeyed every word of the family members like a pet dog. Biren and Naren marvelled at the ease with which she was being domesticated. But as men of the world, they had their reservations. A tiger could never be believed. They could turn hostile at the slightest provocation. They are, again, bound to behave in strange manner when there would be a breeding season. The cage had been ordered.

Another tragedy occurred. Sharbari, alias Angelina died in spite of all the expert supervision. The vet was of the opinion that it could be because of constant captivity of the animal. Blackwell was heartbroken. He was to go back to Wales in another week. He had started imagining the glamour attached to keeping a tiger in captivity. His stature would have been elevated manifold to his countrymen. But that was not to be.

"Do you understand the implications of keeping a tiger as a pet?" Blackwell told Biren Dutta with all the authority he could master, "A tiger is going to be a threat to your neighbours as well as to your own family. The children, who love this tigress, are themselves at great danger. Who knows the moods of a tiger? Supposing some of your neighbours complain to the police? You are a decent businessman Mr. Dutta, how long you can fight all these menaces? On the other hand, I suggest you to hand over the tigress to me. We, the Europeans have a way to deal with tougher situations like this. I have got a large estate at Wales and there are plenty of people to take care of. You hand me over the tigress and get rid of all the troubles. I am even willing to pay a decent amount for the animal if you like."

Biren himself wanted to get rid of the tigress. For him it was a burden. He was an ordinary forest contractor and was not interested in names born of undue reasons. "I would love to hand the tigress over to you Sir, and the question of money does not arise seeing the type of relation we shared so far. My only concern is the children. They are rather fond of the tigress and it will be difficult to make them part with it."

"I agree," nodded Blackwell, "but mere sentiment is not enough to nurture a tiger. We have to be a little stern in the beginning. Ultimately it will be to their benefit only."

Biren had made up his mind. He would be a strict senior if needed to be. "When are you planning to leave for Wales, Sir?" he asked.

"Just in a couple of days. I will move to Bombay by train and from there I have booked my tickets for a voyage by ship."

"Please make your arrangements for taking Varnamala with you while you are leaving. I assure you that there will be no problem from any of my family members." Biren was stern and determined while declaring the same. Blackwell left pleased, patting his own back for putting up a decisive argument.

Biren did his bit at home. "I have allowed you to keep the tigress for so long only caring your feelings. Now I think enough is enough. We are going to hand over Varnamala to Mr. Blackwell and he will take her to Wales with him. It is not the job of us, the ordinary Indians to keep a tiger. Let it go to someone who can take real care of her. Get it clear that my decision is final and there will be no amendment to this." These were his words to the children. They understood that their honeymoon with the tigress was over. They knew that something of this nature was due someday or other. They lowered their head and kept quiet.

Blackwell came to Biren's house in the morning of his departure. He came prepared with a large cage and a trained hunter. The feline refused to move and roared. The hunter waved his whip and moved Varnamala to the cage and shut the door of the cage. Varnamala looked at the members of the house in desperation. The atmosphere was poignant. The children could not bear to see the scene and moved inside the house. None of the ladies had a dry eye. A member of the house was being taken away. Blackwell avoided looking at the faces of the household members. He did not want to be soft. To an Englishman, a business is a business. He moved away with the cage with the hunter at his toe.

The incidence has haunted Achintya many a time in his life. *Could Biren not keep the tigress with him? He had the money and the infrastructure. The only thing he lacked was a will to do something new. Same was the scenario everywhere in this country.* As was told earlier,

Achintya, by no means was a nationalist or a patriot. On the other hand, he had a deep sense of reverence for the English. They had the courage to think original. Or else, we would not have developed such a solid network of railways or postal services in our country. The English have their ways!

The discussion in Achintya's drawing room had taken a turn on a less controversial event. It was cricket. The debate was about who was a better captain of India? Dhoni or Ganguly? Achintya smiled to himself. *Wasn't cricket also brought to this country by the English?* The English surely have their ways!

THE LIVING GODDESS

Dhanpuri is a drab coalfield town, that is, if you can call it a town at all. Geographically, it is in district Shahdol in the state of Madhya Pradesh. Any standard map of India does not locate it. Yet it is there, studded with coalfields, both open cast and underground. The local economy rotates around coal mining; the shops, the banks, the thefts and the coal mafias. The roads are dusty, the lanes are dingy. Yet there are the offices, the buildings and there is a Central Hospital. It used to be my workplace, about fifteen years back; when I was forty, in 1998 or thereabout. I am a doctor and I am afraid, not a good one. There are hundreds of average doctors in India who find their refuge in various mines or industries. As a general duty doctor, I had to do ward rounds, outdoors as well as emergency duties. Ours being a central hospital, there were as many as thirty doctors in our 150 bedded hospital. All of us did our jobs to the best of our ability. But sometimes, a feeling of monotony used to get over me and I craved to get away from everything. I am not sure whether things were like this with others as well, but at such times I was in search of a leeway. It is difficult, with your friends and family encircling you like a barrier. However, it was possible for a short span on some occasions.

My escaping instincts were troubling me for some time those days. Then suddenly I encountered a holiday. Maybe it was a Sunday, I don't remember. That winter morning, after getting up late, I discovered that I did not have many important things to do. The ward rounds took exactly half an hour and it was followed by a quick visit to the market purchasing vegetables and livestock good enough to last an entire week. It was about eleven in the morning and by holiday standards I guessed the lunch to be about three hours away. So I caught hold of my old scooter that was always willing to carry me on these weird trips and started off for the unknown. My wife, not being of a nagging nature, did not bother me with questions like where I was going or when I would be back. She was aware of my periodic nomadic ventures and knew well that the homing pigeon would be back to its abode whenever the sojourn was over.

My faithful old scooter rattled through the lanes of Dhanpuri with its rightful owner on its back. After moving aimlessly for a while, I was intrigued by an area called *Villius no. 1*. Not that the place was great

71

looking or something; it was the name, or the apparent inane nature of the name that attracted me enough to make a halt there. It contained some miners' quarters along with private housings. Along the narrow lanes were the usual paraphernalia like shops, a mosque, a post office and some vehicles. A shabby looking teashop offered me some hope for a cup of tea. The tea was in the suspected line of hopelessness. I sipped it nonchalantly. There were not much customers in the shop. An elderly Muslim fellow was sitting in front of me with a local news paper in his hand. Knelling of bell and devotional songs were being heard at a distance.

I did not notice when an old woman had appeared near my bench. She looked shrivelled and crippled. She wore a torn and dirty sari with several patchworks of mending and a wrapper, which looked no better than a rag, was turned around the upper half of her body. Her lean body was stooped and she could not walk. She was just dragging her body with the help of both her hands. Her age was difficult to guess, but I figured it to be anywhere above seventy. I thought her to be a beggar, but she did not ask for anything. She only kept looking at me blankly.

I consider me to be smart enough to tackle a given situation. But there are moments I am at a loss as to how to react. This was one such occasion. Before I could realise how to respond to the old woman, my fellow tea-drinker from the opposite bench got up and offered an *aloo-bonda* to the old woman. It was a great sight that followed. Her eyes lightened at the sight of the snack. She then started caressing the *aloo-bonda* lovingly as if it was a new born child and started humming something softly. Then she opened it into two pieces carefully and smelt it leaving heaving a pleasurable sigh. It was followed by eating bit by bit. The glistening in her eyes told that she was enjoying every bit of the pieces of potato mixture and the overlying gram flour coat which she ate slowly. *Aloo-bonda* is a very common snack all over India which is made of a mixture of mashed potato and condiments of the size of small cakes and deep fried in oil with an overlying coat of gram powder. It comes cheap and is known by various names like *aloo-chop, batata-vada* etc. in different parts of the country. I have never seen a happiness of this magnitude while having a simple thing like this. But then, did not they say; happiness is a state of mind? It has nothing to do with the elements of happiness. I felt ashamed. How often we lost our happiness over trivial!

I looked at the man who offered the *aloo-bonda*. The elderly Muslim fellow looked at the old woman with a kind of adoration. "Isn't she happy?" he expressed, looking at me.

"Of course, she is," I smiled as well. "Should I offer her another one?" I asked rather chivalrously."

"I don't think that to be a good idea. Her stomach cannot take more. She will fall ill. I know her long enough not to give her more in spite of her zeal for oily snacks." The fellow was authoritative in saying so.

"Who is she?" I asked.

"Oh, she is just a *pagli* (an insane woman). No one cares for her, may be except this Rashid Siddiqi." He tapped his chest rather remorsefully.

"Rashid bhai, do you know her since long?" this Rashid character looked interesting to me.

"Of course I do, since a reasonable time. But you can care for someone if he or she touches a string in your heart even if you don't know him or her for long. Isn't it so?" Rashid philosophised. I instantly developed a liking for the person.

"You are absolutely right," I smiled and extended my right hand to him. "I am Doctor Sanjay Singh."

"Doctor Sahib!" his eyes widened as he took my hand. I was not averse to this kind of revered expressions as I met the commoners. But the question was, was he at all a commoner? By the initial association with him, he did not look like one.

"I work at the local central hospital of the colliery," I said in a casual manner. "Do you live somewhere near?"

"Yes sir, my house is in this Villius No. 1 itself. I have made a small house after my retirement. I was a driver in the colliery," then Rashid added with an air of pride, "I used to drive the jeep of a sub area manager."

Sub area managers are big shots in colliery in their own right. "How about one more cup of tea?" I asked.

"Sure, provided you allow me to pay for it. You are, after all, a guest to my area." Rashid had a sense of pride.

I did not object. Over the next cup of tea, the conversation took an easy turn. It started with our subject of introduction, the *pagli,* or the old woman.

"You know, the pagli has lost her memory completely," said Rashid. "She stays in the local Rani Devi temple since long. No one takes any notice of her. I have developed a liking for her. In spite of losing her memory, she seems to be dignified enough. I have never seen her begging for anything. Sometime someone offers her a cloth and she accepts it gleefully. If someone offers her food, she takes it; or else she doesn't complain. She must be from a decent family."

"Does anybody know where she comes from, if she is not from the locality?" I asked the pertinent question.

There was a mysterious smile that flashed on Rashid's lips. It was barely visible through the depth of white beard and whisker that he sported. "No, no one has any idea where she comes from. But I am seeing her in and around the temple since last five years or so."

I looked at the pagli. She was slowly dragging herself away crutching on both her hands. It was time I thought we must change over to some better subject.

"Rashid bhai, can you tell why this area is called a Villius? I believe there are two more like this as well. I had always been curious to know it."

"That's a good question," Rashid appreciated with a nod, "I am sure many of the local residents are not aware of it. You must know this coalfield belonged to the Shaw-Wallace group before."

"Till 1973 I think, when it was taken over by the Government of India by the coal mines nationalisation act," I said.

"Yes, during the regime of Mrs. Indira Gandhi." Rashid seemed to appreciate my general awareness. "Before nationalisation, there used to be agents in the areas instead of the present day general managers. They were the sole representatives of the owner of the mines. That is why they used to be all powerful in a coal belt. John Williams was such an agent who came here around 1950. He was an excellent young man from Ireland. In addition to being a strict agent, he was a man with a difference."

"Difference?" I interrupted.

"Yes, he had a great heart, unlike the others. The agents prior to him were only interested in digging out coal. But Williams thought of the welfare of the coal miners as well. Earlier, the miners used to stay in *dhaodas* (shoddy mud built houses). He first thought of building *pucca* houses for them. That was the time he built three colonies for miners and they were named after him only. It was Williams' 1, 2 and 3 respectively. Over the years, through corruption of pronunciation of the locals, William's has become Villius." Rashid stopped with a smile.

I could not help smiling myself. It is funny how some changes take place, I thought. "Your Williams was smart though," I told Rashid. "Modern concept of management also suggests that the productivity of an industry increases manifold when you keep the people comfortable."

"Not only that," Rashid was encouraged, "it was difficult for a person from Ireland to pick up the local dialect, but within a couple of years Williams picked up Hindi as well as the local dialect with ease. He used to communicate well with his people in the mines. That is why he was very successful as an agent. He even got married to a local girl. She was from Rewa."

"That's interesting," I said, seeing the turn of events going towards a love angle.

May be Rashid got such an intrigued audience after a long time. He continued his narration with zeal. "I was barely 15 0r 16 those days. It should be around 1955." He looked skywards as he tried to recollect. I figured he was right. We were in 2005 and Rashid did not look more than sixty-five. "Williams went on some business trip to Rewa, as I have heard from my father at a later date."

"Was your father also employed in colliery?" I asked.

"Yes, he was a loader in the mines. He was uneducated," reminisced Rashid. Then he added proudly, "I was the first one to go to school in my family. Those days we had to go all the way to Shahdol to attend to school. Later on, a school was started here by Williams Sahib himself. I studied up to class nine."

Seeing him deviating from the topic I had to make a gentle interruption. "You were talking of the marriage of Williams."

"Yes, he went on some business trip to Rewa." Rashid resumed, "It is said that he met one Mr. Jaiswal over there who was a tycoon of some sort. Rani Devi was Mr. Jaiswal's daughter. Her name was something else during that time. It was after her marriage she became Rani. Devi was the suffix she got much later."

"Did they get married soon after the business meet?"

"Well they got married soon after, but it was not the usual kind of marriage. She eloped with Williams."

"Eloped? Was there any problem?" I asked.

"Of course there were. The Jaiswals were a conservative family and Rani's marriage was already fixed with a boy of their own caste. In addition, rumours went that Williams was married to an English lady whom he had abandoned for some reason. Yet, love can behave strangely and the two of them eloped within a month of their first meeting."

"There must have been a great commotion over the issue," I suggested, as I was getting involved in the past.

"There was, but these things get diluted over time. They got married in the court and a ceremony followed in which all the people of the area were invited. As a young boy I also witnessed the ceremony. The couple looked gorgeous. It was since that time she was called 'Rani', the wife of the king of the area. You know, the agents were no less than kings in their coalfields. I started addressing her as Rani Didi like many other in the area. But I must admit, on the day of feast I was more interested in the grand menu than admiring the couple. Forty goats were sacrificed for the guests." Rashid remembered with relish.

"Did anyone from Rani's paternal side attend the feast?" I still hoped that a last minute patch up job might have been made.

"No question of that," ascertained Rashid, "on the other hand, her parents and folks disowned any responsibility to her. They never saw her face again."

I did not know when I started feeling for the Rani. A lone girl getting married to an Irish and abandoned by her people; must had been tough on her. "I hope she was happy after marriage," I uttered involuntarily.

Rashid seemed happy that I asked this question. "Not only was she happy, she tried to make everyone around her happy. She was initially taken by Williams to his official bungalow, but she liked to stay with the common men and that was when Williams built her a house in this very Villius. It is a large house which is still there. First turn on the left of this lane will take you there. Rani Didi was educated in college and she opened a school for the girls of this area in the outhouse of the building. Then she started self help group amongst the local women where they were taught to make homemade food products and sell them through a co-operative."

This must have been the older version of the present day ladies' club, I thought. In my heart, I loathed the way they functioned though. I had seen the ladies coming well dressed in medical camps, distributing fruits and blankets to the poor only to be photographed for the newspapers while caressing a poor child. I strongly suspected that they washed their hands thoroughly with detergent as soon as they reached their houses. In my mind I started revering the Rani. Then I suddenly remembered.

"Didn't you say there is a local Rani Devi temple around where the pagli stays?"

"Yes, it is the shelter to not only the pagli, but to a few beggars as well. Have you never heard of the temple?" asked Rashid.

I was ashamed that in spite of my reasonably good general awareness, I knew very little around the locality I worked since last five years. I admitted so. "I would like to visit the temple," I added.

"Then I will show you around, if you have got time. It is few minutes' walk from here." Rashid got up from the bench.

We followed the sound of the devotional songs coming from some distance. As we walked I asked, "Is it the same Rani Devi we were talking about?" Rashid confirmed that it was the same one. I marvelled at the ease with which we confer the status of God to a person in our midst. Sometimes a social worker, sometimes a saint, and even a movie star at times! Then, there must be some quality in the person. I thought of asking about this at a later period. Meanwhile, I figured people might be disillusioned of mythical gods at times and search for something more tangible for a change.

Within five minutes we reached the temple. It was a small one with a reasonable cemented arena. The temple was situated at one end of the arena with 'Rani Devi Temple' inscribed on its dome in Hindi. The year of establishment was beside it. It was 1970. Only thirty-five years from now, I calculated. There were two tin shades on both side of the temple with one having a make shift oven. The other one, having a few cemented benches, was for the devotees to wait. There was an extension of the temple proper with tiled floor and roof which was used for different religious rituals. A deep well with a subjacent room, possibly for the priest completed the set up. There must have been some occasion on that day which accounted for a sizable number of devotees, mostly females, offering their prayers. I did not see the foreseen pagli anywhere. I wondered where she stayed.

To my surprise, Rashid entered the temple with folded hands and offered his prayer to the deity and followed it with knelling of the brass bell in the extension of the temple. Dhanpuri has a sizable number of Muslim populations and communal harmony was the norm. But to see a Muslim offering his devotion in a pure Hindu way did puzzle me to some extent. Then I saw some other Muslims, male and female alike doing the same thing as well. I followed them with similar mannerism.

"How did your Rani Didi reached 'Devi' status?" I showed my curiosity as we relaxed, sitting on one of the benches.

Rashid had a quizzical smile on his heavily bearded face. "Lot of people, who came from outside, were surprised with the ease with which the Hindus and the Muslims gel at this temple. I figure you are no exception to that. Both the community have lived together since ages. We have our cultural differences alright, at the same time we respect each other's traditions. We haven't allowed people with vested interest to insinuate in our living. Then, the people of this area have a religion in common; that is, we all are miners. That is how this temple came into being. Rani Didi used to go inside the mines and she used to gather a firsthand knowledge of the plight of the miners inside it. She had insisted on a better working condition in the mines. Not to speak of the innumerable social reforms she introduced. This deep sense of reverence has given her the 'Devi' status. You can say she is the goddess of mine."

I heard about a goddess of forests, but the concept of a goddess of mines was new to me. While inside the temple, I had a glimpse of the deity in it. It was a medium sized marble statue of a female adorned with a crown. But as usual with the temples, the deity was so heavily smeared with pastes of vermillion and turmeric that it was impossible to differentiate the features of the idol.

I considered of returning back home. Even by my bizarre standards I was getting late. Rashid was decent enough to see me off up to my scooter. While going out of the temple, we saw the pagli entering the temple premises dragging herself with her hands. Her heavily wrinkled ugly face had a contented smile. Like Rashid, I felt a fascination for her as well. Ignorance can be bliss indeed!

"I am personally indebted to Rani Devi," Rashid said, as if to himself as I approached my scooter.

"Is it so?" I turned back to him.

"Yes Doctor Sahib, but that is a rather long story. May be I will tell about it some other day." Rashid was hesitant.

Once I get intrigued by something it is difficult to deter me. Moreover, knowing my effervescence of mood, I was not sure whether I would be able to meet him a second time. I postponed the idea of my departure and sat on the bench of the teashop once more and ordered two more cups of tea along with some freshly fried snacks.

"Let's go on with it," I said with a smile, "I have got the time if you have."

Rashid was pleased that I had found time for his story. Might be he was in search of an interested audience which he did not get for some time.

"My father died when I was barely nineteen. I had left school sometime back and was loitering around. His death came as a shock to us. Those days there were no trade unions and no labour compensation laws. My elder brother had left the house long back and he did not keep any contact with us. I, being the only person at house capable of earning a livelihood, tried my luck at the colliery and other places. No one wanted to hire me. Our condition turned from bad to worse. It was at this time Rani Didi came to our house and saw our plight. On her persuasion to Williams Sahib, I got a job in the colliery. Thereafter, I got a driver's licence and became a driver. Rani Didi was very fond of me and soon I became driver to Williams Sahib himself. Those were the days!" Rashid's eyes glittered as if it happened yesterday only. "Not only me, many houses in the colliery, and particularly in the Villius have such stories," he added afterwards.

I began to appreciate the halloed presence of Rani Devi. But building a temple and offering regular prayers were still a bit of exaggeration to me. For the time being, I thought to drop the topic of Rani Devi. "What happened to Williams finally? Did he stay here up to the nationalisation of the coal mines?" I asked.

"No," said Rashid, "He was taken off his position long before the nationalisation. A *desi* agent was posted in his place. He did not go back to Europe after that. He stayed back here, in the Villius. He rather loved the people over here." Rashid gushed out a sigh. "His end was pathetic though," Rashid added as a corollary.

"What happened to him?" I asked in an earnest manner.

Rashid lowered his head. "It was all our fault. In the year 1970, some Muslim religious leaders visited the local mosque. They were successful in their own way to inculcate hatred for the Hindus in the mind of the local Muslims. This brought into action a small scale riot amongst the two communities. Williams Sahib went to the centre of the action to put an end to this. The riot stopped alright, but Williams lost his life in the process." Rashid made a remorseful pause and then continued. "Communal tension never aroused its ugly head following that, but that came at a big price."

"What happened to Rani Devi?" I asked.

"She became a *sati*." Rashid smiled sadly.

I was startled. I thought *sati* system of dying in the funeral pyre of husband was abolished long back, during the era of Raja Ram Mohan Roy. I expressed so.

"It was not the usual funeral pyre thing." Rashid dismissed my idea. "After the religious rights of Williams were performed, it was done as per Hindu belief; Rani Didi went to Amarkantak to offer prayer to Lord Shiva. Have you been to Amarkantak?"

Amarkantak, with a few temples and shrines on the Vindhya and Satpura ranges is about 80 kilometres from the place and the main attractions of it are the origins of the rivers Narmada and Sone. It was one of my favourite tourist spots as well.

"I took Rani Didi along with five to six other females and a priest to Amarkantak. While coming back from the source of the Narmada, she ordered me to take the vehicle towards *Sonemuda*, the origin of the Sone. It happened there," said Rashid.

"What happened?" I asked with baited breath.

"It was raining that day," went on Rashid, "the waterfall at Sonemuda was in full flow and so was the current in the rivulet underneath. Rani Didi along with the other ladies stood on the observatory over the waterfall. Suddenly she started behaving in an odd manner. She started chanting something like, 'here he comes, see how pale he has gone, he needs me,' and before anybody could realise a thing she jumped in the waterfall. Nothing was heard beyond her long shriek in the falls. We immediately called the attention of the locals and the help of some divers was taken. Nothing was found on that day. It was only after three days, her swollen body, clad in white was recovered near a village about 20 kilometres away. Then onwards, she was called Rani Devi. Some even call her Sati Devi." He came to a stop.

That is more viable an explanation for godhood, I thought. Then finally I got up and started for home. Throughout the day, the story of Rani Devi remained reverberant in my heart. Even I told the story to my wife. She was fascinated as well.

Over the days that followed, Rani Devi, Williams and Rashid Siddiqi gradually trickled out of my mind. I became engrossed in my daily routine. Once, while on night duty, the ward boy from the male medical ward came to call me to attend to a patient. "The old man is vomiting blood," he said.

The man indeed was in a precarious state. He looked thin with prominent Adam's apple and ribs. His eyes propped out of its sockets because of stress. After providing the emergency treatment, I looked at his case sheet. He was suspected of having lung cancer. A biopsy report was awaited from Tata Cancer Centre. It was a grim situation overall. I looked at the name. It was Rashid Siddiqi! I wished I never met him in person.

"The man wants to talk to you, sir," reported the ward sister.

"Didn't you recognise me Doctor Sahib?" asked Rashid in a horse and tired voice as I reached his bed.

"I did not, at first," I admitted, "as I was going through the case papers I knew it was you."

"No wonder, sir," he managed a faint smile, "I am hardly recognisable these days."

"Please don't strain yourself by talking too much," I held his hands in an effort to console him. "We can talk when you get well."

"May be the Allah does not wish so." He continued to speak. "I am suffering from cancer and my days are limited. It is urgent for me to speak something; or else it may remain untold. Won't you listen?" *he knew it.*

The eagerness in his voice urged me to sit on a stool beside his bed.

"I did not tell you the entire truth." Rashid said as he cleared his throat.

"About what?" I did not guess the line he was about to take up.

He looked around. There was hardly a soul in the ward who was awake in the middle of night. He went on with his narration clearing his throat. Though he strained initially, I could hear every word precisely. It was as intriguing as it was startling. I listened intently without interruption.

It was about Rani Devi. Three days after Rani Devi jumped off from Sonemuda, Rashid went back to the spot; just to pay his last regards to her. While returning back, he stopped for a cup of tea at a local shop. There he overheard a conversation between two persons about some lady being rescued by the sages in Jaleshwar Dham shrine three days' back. Curious, he went on to the Jaleshwar Dham to see his Rani Didi lying over there. As he was thrilled to see the development, she went forward to talk to her, but there was a blank look in her face. One of the hermits informed him that she had lost her memory completely due to the fall. She would not be able to recognise any of the faces she knew so long. Furthermore, she had a severe trauma on her back which resulted in paralysis of both her legs. "I was in a state of shock, doctor sahib. I thought she would better be dead than living like this," told Rashid. But the sages told that there were chances that her condition would improve further. Dejected, he came back. He did not tell anybody about this.

"Don't you think, you should have told others about this so that she could be taken to a good hospital for better health care?" I interjected at this point.

"May be it was my fault," Rashid pondered, "but us, the common men of this region have a different mindset. By that time she was already hailed as a *sati* and was given the status of a goddess amongst the locals. Making of her temple was being planned with full enthusiasm along with devotional songs made in her name being sung at various places. How could I bring her down from her place of glory? Moreover, we believe more in sages and godmen than doctors in treating such cases. Later on, as time progressed, I thought there might be better ways of handling it. But by then, it was too late."

Rashid was dejected and distraught as he could neither reveal the truth to others, nor see the enthusiastic devotional march of the people in this regard. He managed a transfer to another coalfield in Orissa and worked there for twenty years till his retirement. During this period he visited the Jaleshwar Dham shrine from time to time. There was some physical improvement in her condition, but the two basic problems remained untouched. She moved with the help of her hands and sometimes offered a helping hand to the sages in arranging the flowers or offerings to the God. It was about ten years after his retirement, that is, five years from now he came to know that the *Mohanta,* or the chief hermit of the shrine had passed away and the new one was reluctant to keep Rani Devi in the shrine. That was when he brought Rani Devi back to Villius. She had become too old to be recognised by then.

"Did you keep her at your house then?" I asked.

"I wish I could," repented Rashid, "but I could not have my own ways at my house then. My wife had died prior to that and my house was ruled by my son and daughter in law. Who would take the extra burden of an old woman? I thought it better to keep her at the place where she belonged, her own temple."

"What happened to her house?" I inquired. "Was there nobody to look after her?"

"House!" Rashid emitted a wry smile. "What used to be the abode of many homeless people, turned into a junkyard soon. Her only son had left for England long back, never to return. He did not inherit the quality of either of the parents. Soon after the news of death of Rani Devi a score of claimants from her parental side reached the house to put claim on the property. Rani Devi lost all her property and the house was rented to three occupants dividing it into three parts. I am left with very little money myself and there is a restrain on me on spending that either; such is the curse of old age." Tears started dripping from the eyes of Rashid. "Yet I try to provide her with whatever I can within my limited resources."

I had guessed it a little while back. Yet I wanted to be sure. "So, it was the pagli we were talking of, isn't it?"

82

"Yes, it is." Rashid was still sobbing. "You remain only the second person after me to know the truth about Rani Devi. I am afraid you are soon going to be the only one after my death. I am sure I can count on you to keep it within you."

How on the earth can I divulge a thing like this to others? I could not be that insensitive. I told him as much. He was seemingly relieved. I wondered at the unexpected turns of life that one has to encounter. Such romantic feelings! At that moment I promised to Rashid that I would look after the 'pagli' to the best of my ability till her last day. He clasped my hands it gratitude. His eyes said it all.

Unlike many decisions taken by me at the height of emotion, I did not repent this one. There was a sense of bliss that worked on me while taking care of Rani Devi. I bribed a female assistant of the priest of Rani Devi temple into looking after the pagli. I provided her with fresh clothes and fixed an allowance for her food. The assistant was assured of better sum if I was satisfied with her service. In our country, nothing works like a bribe. The assistant washed her up and dressed her. The pagli looked better than before. I wondered whether there was any semblance in her with her old self. But Rashid, who only could have answered my curiosity, was not to be seen for more than a month. I assumed that either he was transferred to a bigger hospital, or was dead by then. I was satisfied that I could keep my words given to him. I had developed an affinity towards the pagli; may be of a lesser intensity than that of Rashid.

One evening, as I was looking at the pagli eating a piece of cake with immense satisfaction, someone told from my back, "I couldn't have done this much. Doctor Sahib, you have done a great job!"

I looked back with a start. It was Rashid! He had recovered well and was nearly back to his old self. "Allah Mian did not accept me this time. It turned out to be some chest infection rather than cancer." He smiled at me gleefully. "The secret has to be shared within two of us for some more time."

I was so glad to see back Rashid in his old form. I embraced him. "Isn't two better than one?" I said.

The pagli was looking blankly at her own idol in the heart of the temple.

<hr>

THE RETURN INVITATION

"Make yourself available in the evening. Will you?" Bidisha Sanyal told her husband. Probir could not make out whether it was a command or a request. In his long conjugal life, twenty-four years to be exact, with Bidisha, Probir has failed to make out the mood of Bidisha on many occasions under similar circumstances in the past.

"Depends on the nature of emergencies that arrive in the hospital in the evening." Probir removed his shoes and went on to catch hold of a towel. He wanted to have a refreshing shower. He already has had a tough day at the hospital. It was 2 PM and he had just returned from the morning session at the hospital. The afternoon session starts at four and he wanted to have a relaxing nap following his lunch before going to hospital again.

"That's why I have informed you in advance so that you can adjust your things accordingly. It is urgent." There was a note of seriousness in Bidisha.

"Is it?" Probir stopped on his way from the anteroom, "How urgent exactly?" He knew that the urgency of his spouse could range from buying cosmetics to attend the marriage anniversary of one of her ladies' club pals.

"We have to go to the GM's house." Bidisha said somewhat desperately.

"GM's house! Why on the earth?" It was a shocker to Probir. The General Manager is the top administrator in the Area and the other officers prefer to keep a safe distance from him. Dr. Probir Sanyal is working in the coal belt hospitals since last seventeen years, and he has never met the GM unless he was called upon to meet him. On the top of that, in spite of his reasonably long service in the industry, he remains in the rank of mid level executive. This is, partly attributable to the slow rate of promotion in the medical discipline compared to others, and partly due to his joining late in the organisation. This is Probir's third job.

Not that Bidisha was not aware of these facts; but she did not have any other way out. Dussehra had ended only a few days' back. The Bengalis observe Dussehra as Bijoya Dashami. The officers' wives in the ladies' club of Bishrampur Area had a get together a couple of days' back to celebrate Bijoya Dashami. This was done, as the General Manager at present is Aniruddha Majumdar, a Bengali person. This is another norm in the colliery belt, which Probir failed to understand. The culture and norms in the colliery areas run as per the likes and dislikes of its respective general managers. There is no preset rule. If the GM is vegetarian, all the parties are devoid of any non-vegetarian dish. If the GM is a fitness freak, the Area gyms are replenished with latest fitness kits and all the senior executives in the Area turn into exercise lovers. Conversely, the same senior colliery officials would turn into regular boozers if the next GM happened to be fond of liquor. If the men follow the GM, the ladies are not far behind either. Charulata, GM's wife and the first lady of the area is an ardent follower of Bengali culture. Therefore, Bijoya-Dashami was celebrated with fervour by the ladies in the club. It was there Bidisha was asked to sing a Tagore song. Not that she sings very well, but during her school and college days, she used to sing Tagore songs in which she had some formal training. After long years of being away from music, Bidisha's voice has become rusty. Yet she sings occasionally, as she sang that night. At the end of the function, Charulata, and Anjana, the wife of Deputy GM Mr. Dutta had praised Bidisha a lot and expressed their desire to come to Bidisha's quarter to listen to more songs from her. Bidisha was seemingly overwhelmed by the situation and called them for lunch on next Sunday. She had done her part; now it was for Probir to go to the houses of these two heavy weights, of course along with Bidisha, and invite the ladies along with their respective husbands for dinner on Sunday. Incidentally, Sukumar Dutta, the Dy. GM is also a Bengali.

To his dismay, the post lunch nap that Probir had contemplated earlier, could not take place. There was a call from the Chief Medical Officer, Dr. Jha that an IOD was on its way from the mines to the hospital and Probir was to report immediately to the hospital. IOD, or Injured on Duty is a serious thing in the mines. The Sub Area Managers and the GM have a heck of a time explaining the lapse of safety precautions taken in the mines to their respective seniors. In addition, there are the trade union leaders and the reporters from print as well as electronic media. They complete the scenario with their presence and diversity of opinion. Overall, the entire conundrum has to be managed efficiently and diplomatically. That is why Probir is called. He is not a specialist; but he has worked in the department of trauma and bony injuries for a considerable time. Add to that, his long-standing experience in dealing with public of colliery region. Probir is called to attend the critical cases along with the surgical specialist. Probir got ready within minutes and reached the hospital.

Bishrampur Central Hospital is not a big one as the name might suggest. There are 75 beds in all at the hospital. An operation theatre suffices only for some minor surgeries. There is also a shortage of various technical staffs in the hospital. The CMO, Dr. Jha is not very keen on keeping critically ill cases in the hospital either. As Probir reached the hospital, he saw the GM already at the porch waiting for the patient to arrive.

"Good afternoon sir." Probir had to wish him.

"I don't see anything good about the afternoon." Aniruddha Majumdar, the GM was not in a benevolent mood at all. "As far as I heard of the incident, the man's right leg has been severed by fall of a heavy stone from the roof."

"We have heard similarly, sir." Probir was polite in his manner.

"All I want is, the man should not loss any part of his limb." Majumdar put up his decree.

"Well sir, it depends on how much of vitality the severed part is left with." Probir was desperate to infuse some sense of logic to the incidence.

"There are several modalities of treatment available these days. We will send the person to the highest possible centre. I don't want any nonsense in this." The entire small stature of Majumdar, along with its potbelly and oversized moustache vibrated vigorously as he gushed out his announcement. He wanted to make his statement public. Dr. Jha, standing by his side, nodded appreciatively. Probir realised that one of the local TV reporters was making a video recording. He advanced towards the casualty to join the surgeon and others in the treatment team.

The injury sustained by the person was a bad one. He was a middle-aged person named Sitaram. His right leg was almost severed at about six inches above the ankle. There was heavy bleeding from the injury and the bones were broken. The injured part of the limb was dangling precariously from the proximal part. Necessary treatment was given to him and Sitaram was despatched to Apollo Hospital Bilaspur for further management. Tranquillity was brought back to the small colliery hospital for the time being. The GM went back keeping his dignity intact.

"Are you sure you want to invite the GM for lunch?" Probir asked Bidisha in the evening. He was half-hopeful that Bidisha might change her plan on a second thought. That was not to be.

"Why shouldn't I? Moreover, what makes you bother that much? It is, after all a personal lunch gathering with two Bengali families and we will have a little bit of cultural programme." Bidisha remained unperturbed. "In fact, it is I who should be bothering. I have to cook the food and I have to sing most of the songs," she smiled.

"I realise that perfectly well," said Probir, still perturbed, "but the fact remains that they are the two heavy weights of this area. In case you don't realise it, let me tell you that these people never consider us their equals. It is only your grade and seniority that matters to them. I don't mind as long as a person is good at heart; but with these people I doubt whether they have such an organ at all." Probir usually avoids discussing official matters and protocols with his wife, but on this occasion, he went on. "If they agree to lunch with you, they would come with the air of gracing your house with their presence. Moreover, our neighbours will get envious and accuse us of sycophancy. I am not worrying for nothing."

Bidisha did not realise that so many intricacies could be attached to a simple thing like calling someone for lunch. She also knew how much her husband hated sycophancy. He is known to be an upright man and have never taken to any unfair means to get any untoward benefit from his superiors.

"Alright," she said quietly, "since I have already committed myself, just support me this time. This will never be repeated."

Probir kept quiet for some time. He knew that he had to oblige his wife. "I think you have to take an appointment from the GM to meet him at his home as per his availability," he said at last.

"That I have already arranged." Bidisha put up a big smile. "I have asked Charulata madam to call us when the GM is back at home. She has said that tonight GM will be back by about 9.30 PM and she will call as soon as he arrives."

Probir marvelled at the ease with which women arrange the things. Bidisha added as an afterthought, "Of course Anjana didi helped."

This, Probir thought, *is the essential difference. Charulata is GM's wife and hence a madam always. Anjana is deputy GM's wife and she can be called a 'didi'.* But he had overlooked another fact; the GM is new to the area whereas the Mr. Dutta, his deputy is in the area since quite some time.

However, the expected call from the wife of the GM did not arrive by quarter to ten at night. Bidisha called again.

"I was about to give you a call Bidisha," Charulata Majumdar quipped at the other end; "he has come back just now and is getting fresh. You can come now."

Another trick at unnecessary hype, thought Probir.

The GM's bungalow looked like a castle as Probir's car entered the gate. There were two security men at the gate. Then was a well-lit driveway that led to the car park. One more security there. Then a small walk to the front door, provided with another security personnel. Probir did not fail to notice three official vehicles parked at the private parking of the GM. *What a royal life!* Wondered Probir.

Mrs. Majumdar was there at the door herself to receive the couple. She was cordial in her welcome. Probir and Bidisha were made to sit in the drawing room. Soon Aniruddha Majumdar joined the party.

"Dr. Sanyal, if I remember correctly?" He shook his hand with Probir. And then folded his hands to Bidisha.

"That's right sir," told Probir as he took the hand of the GM. *Such a show off! He remembers me perfectly. Only this afternoon we met.* He was taking mental notes as well.

"So, what do you make of that IOD patient? Is his leg going to survive?" Majumdar was casual in his approach. Probir, however, kept quiet.

Majumdar smiled. He was no fool. "I am asking a frank opinion, Dr. Sanyal. You need not have to be formal while answering."

Probir felt better. Yet he was cautious. "As far as my opinion goes, chances are remote. In fact, I have talked to the treating surgeon at the Apollo Hospital. He has kept him on an external fixator."

"What on the earth is that?"

"It is a device in which the bones are fixed in their position and the soft tissue is taken care of. If the tissue healing is satisfactory, a second operation is planned at a later stage so salvage the limb. But having known the case, the chances of healing of the soft tissues are few and far between." Probir was sincere in his opinion.

"Then why the hell are they lingering on?" Majumdar was as forceful as ever.

"Sir, the doctor has to make every effort to save the limb."

"Or, is it an effort to increase the hospital bill at the company's expense? The doctors leave no leaf unturned to inflate their pockets." It seemed Majumdar had forgotten that he was sitting in front of a doctor. He always considered doctors of the company to be only the employees of the same.

"There are aberrations to the general rule, sir. But yet most of them are sincere enough." Probir made a gentle protest.

Snacks and tea were served in the meantime. Majumdar requested them to have snacks and took his own cup of tea.

"Look at Dr. Prabhakaran and Dr. Mishra for that matter," Majumdar was still lingering on the topic of doctors, "they earn a lot from the private patients. I think they are to be served with a reminder that private practice is banned in our organisation."

Probir did not say anything in reply. Prabhakaran and Mishra were the physician and the dentist respectively in their hospital. They indeed had a good amount of patients who are not colliery employees. But it was none of their fault. They never invited the patients; the patients came as they found these doctors good. And he saw no harm if they take their professional fees for spending their personal time for the patients. Of course, private practice is legally not allowed in the company, but no one is serious about such laws. *And look at this GM!* Thought Probir, *he has so many dubious sources of income amounting to astronomical sum; and he speaks of the doctors! A person living in glasshouse should not throw stone at others'.* In this organisation, things remain like this. He sighed. He wished the matter of invitation got over soon so that he could leave.

The two ladies, however, were busy with the talks on their favourite TV serials. Charulata turned towards her husband scornfully. "Will you keep talking of your office at your home as well? They have come to make a personal request to you."

"Sir, I came to request you and madam to have lunch with us at our place on coming Sunday." He parroted out to the questioning glance of Majumdar as was planned with Bidisha. Then added in the same breath, "Mr. And Mrs. Dutta will also be there."

The manner in which Majumdar did not ask any question suggested that he was informed of the same beforehand by his wife.

"Let me see," he made a mental calculation, "isn't it the same day I am invited to preside over the closing ceremony of the DAV public school?" Last part of his statement was made for his wife.

Charulata caught hold of an invitation letter from a shelf nearby and turned over the pages. "Well, it starts at 3.00 PM," she told.

"We will make sure to leave you by that time." Probir was happy inside, as he would get rid of the GM earlier on that day.

"It is done then. Please make sure the food is simple." Majumdar smiled.

It came to the domain of Bidisha by that time. She asserted that the food would remain as per his choice and the discussion turned to food and its intricacies in different parts of the country. An informal atmosphere was created.

As Probir tried to beg leave of the Majumdar couple, both of them vehemently protested. They said that they were late diners and they would enjoy the chat to go on for some more time. Probir sat back reluctantly. It was during this chat Majumdar revealed that he belonged to a very simple family from one of the remote villages in Bengal.

"No one told me that there was something like an entrance examination for professional courses when I passed out from my village school," mused Majumdar; "it was only when I came to Calcutta that someone told me to fill up the forms for the entrance exams. I filled up the forms for both medical and engineering entrance. Interestingly, I got selected for both."

Probir understood two things. Majumdar, in spite of his high position, felt alone at the top. He relished informal talk. At the same time, he loved to brag. In course of conversation, it was also revealed that Probir had done two more services before joining the present one. Majumdar insisted on perseverance with a single job, which can lead a person to the pinnacle, citing his own example.

They stayed at the GM's residence for an hour before leaving. Whereas it was a mixed feeling to Probir, Bidisha enjoyed the sojourn.

Inviting the Deputy GM, Mr. Dutta was however, a much less arduous task. Probir and Bidisha visited them the next evening and the process of invitation was completed in a cordial and homely atmosphere.

There was a hushed excitement at Probir Sanyal's house right from the morning of Sunday. Bed covers were changed in all the rooms, sofa set was adorned with new covers; a carpet, kept for special occasions, was laid on the floor of the drawing room. Add to that minute adjustment like keeping a freshly unpacked soap in a new soap case on the dining hall basin, or special set of crockery being brought into action. Bidisha worked tirelessly doing things herself as well as passing instructions to the housemaid. Almost a festive atmosphere was created. Probir was apprehensive. He hoped against hope that there might be a last minute cancellation of the programme by the GM given the busy nature of his job.

However, nothing unusual happened. At about 1.00 PM Anjana Dutta informed that they were arriving soon and they would be followed by the GM couple in a quarter of an hour. Probir had taken a bath in the morning and put on decent outfit for the occasion. He only had to wait with an expectant air for the arrival of the dignitaries. First to arrive was the Dy. GM couple of Sukumar and Anjana Dutta. Sukumar Dutta was to retire in a couple of months' time. They came driving their own car. Sukumar was athletically built and looked younger than his age. His wife matched him perfectly with a pleasant look about her. The conversation went in an informal line. It was then Probir learnt that Sukumar and the GM, Aniruddha Majumdar studied in the same Shibpur Engineering College. He was also surprised to know that Sukumar was, in fact, four years senior to Aniruddha in the college. But somehow, because of the complicated promotion system of CIL Aniruddha went up the ladder earlier. Probir wondered whether Sukumar would have remained the same homely creature had he been the GM of the area. The chair does curious things to people!

The GM and his wife reached at about quarter to two in the afternoon. Aniruddha Majumdar looked officious even on a private visit. "Sorry to be late doctor, with all these mining affairs to be taken care of," he announced as soon as he debarked from his chauffeur driven official Ambassador Car.

Probir shook hands most humbly and expressed that he was honoured to have him as a guest. In comparison, Charulata seemed to be more informal and homely.

As all of them were conversing over a soft drink, Aniruddha suddenly turned towards Probir. "Doctor, can you inject medicine to dogs?"

Probir was in a dilemma how to react. "Sir, we have been trained to inject medications to human beings only. As far as I know, injecting drugs to dogs is a job of a veterinarian." He was as polite as possible while answering.

Charulata was embarrassed by her husband's question. She wanted to divert the topic. But Aniruddha hung on to it. "Yes, I called a veterinarian to give my Bipasha a shot of antibiotic; but that fellow behaved so inhumanly with Bipasha! So I had to reject him." At this point Charulata cleared that Bipasha was the Labrador bitch they had as a pet. Aniruddha continued, "The area in which I was posted previously, Dr. Pradhan, the anaesthetist used give injections to Bipasha. He was so tender while doing so!"

Probir was at a fix. His first reaction was to turn down the request straightway. Then, the GM was his guest and he did not want to offend him. Moreover, the lady wife of the GM had come on request of his wife, Bidisha. He could not hurt Bidisha as well. He looked at the ladies. Bidisha was looking at the floor. Charulata was visibly embarrassed and Anjana went off the room on some pretext. "Well, if you insist sir, I can give it a try. But I am not good with dogs. Please give me a call when you are at home so that you can hold the dog while I inject the medicine. I will try my best; but I am not sure whether it will be as good as Dr. Pradhan. I am always at your service sir." Probir smiled.

Sukumar Dutta smiled as well. He was impressed in the diplomatic manner in which Probir conducted himself. Even Charulata seemed relieved. Aniruddha, however, was not relented. "Alright, I will make a call in one of the evenings. It may be a bit late because of my schedule. Hope you don't mind."

"Not in the least, sir." Probir was happy that the chapter was coming to an end.

There was a small session of songs in which Bidisha was the main artist with the surprise inclusion of Charulata who sang a modern Bengali song. It was imperative that she used to sing well in her younger days. However, Aniruddha found some mistake in the rhythm in his wife's song and tried to correct it by singing a couple of lines himself. In the process, he made a mess of himself. No one laughed, excepting Charulata. She looked at her husband and made it clear that one cannot be good at everything even if he is the all powerful GM of the area; without uttering a word, of course.

The process of lunch went peacefully. It seemed that the efforts made by Bidisha bore fruit. The guests praised all the cuisines. The conversation turned towards the impending retirement of Mr. Dutta. In the process, Aniruddha asked Probir, "Doctor, there must be some time left before you retire?"

"Not much, sir, I will be retiring in another four and half years' time," Probir said, "I joined this organisation quite late."

"Then we must be of the same age group; I will be retiring by the same time as well." Then Aniruddha suddenly must have realised that he was being more personal to a subordinate of his. "That's good in a way. You don't have to bear the responsibility of being the head of an institution. It drains you away," he added quickly.

You don't have to remind every time that you are the boss, you hydra-head, thought Probir. But he preferred to keep quiet.

Soon after the lunch, there was a call from the Principal of the DAV school enquiring whether the GM would be available to be at the school for the closing ceremony. GM was happy to receive the call and answered in his cell phone that he believed in sticking to his schedule as far as practicable.

"See, now you cannot even have some rest after such a nice lunch." Aniruddha looked at Sukumar Dutta for approval. Sukumar obliged by nodding.

"So, ladies and gentlemen! I will have to leave, as you can see." Aniruddha left as officiously as he had arrived. Probir was thankful to the DAV Principal for giving a timely reminder to the GM.

Sukumar Dutta and Anjana stayed back for some more time and there were more of Tagore songs from Bidisha; this time in a more congenial milieu. The other three also joined their voices from time to time. They left after a cup of tea.

Five years have passed since that time. Coal India Limited, Bishrampur Area and service are things of past to Probir now. His daughter and son, who were studying those days, are in service now. Both are software engineers and the daughter is happily married as well. The son is working in Mumbai. Probir and Bidisha are the only two regular occupants of the three bed roomed flat at Bilaspur, in Chhattisgarh. Probir had purchased the flat an year before his retirement. By the grace of God, Probir is as fit as a nut until this day. He has opened a clinic near his flat at Bilaspur. He sits there for two hours in the morning and for a similar period in the evening. This he does just as a hobby rather than necessity. Because of his treatment skills as well as gentle behaviour, a good number of patients line up in the clinic daily. It was one such evening he was busy seeing patients. It was then Dilip entered the chamber. Dilip is the attendant who sends the patients in as per their allotted numbers.

"Sir, a person wants to meet you without waiting for his turn. He says that you know him and he has to meet you now," Dilip informed.

"Have you asked his name?"

"I did, sir; but he says that it is not necessary."

"He must be crazy. Ask him to wait; or else he might leave the place as well." Probir was busy and he got absorbed in his job once more.

After an hour or so, a short statured man with potbelly and thick, white moustache entered the room. Probir recognised him instantly. He was Aniruddha Majumdar, the past GM of Bishrampur Area. Although recognisable, he looked a pale shadow of the all-important official of the past. He dressed shabbily and stooped a little. Probir got up from his chair and stuck his hand out. "Welcome sir, it is a surprise indeed to see you here."

Aniruddha shook hands and both of them sat down.

"Was it you who wanted to come in earlier?" Probir suddenly remembered.

"Yes, that was me." Aniruddha nodded.

"You should have told your name," complained Probir.

"There," smiled Aniruddha wryly, "I hesitated. You are no more my subordinate. Had you still refused me entry, I'd be hurt. Old habits die hard, as you know."

"Never think of that sir. After all, we had been colleagues in the same area." Probir was as decent as ever.

"That is the point," Aniruddha emphasised, "and this I never realised all my working days. As a GM, I relished my chair and power. People came to me with different requests; legitimate or otherwise. I obliged them. That made them happy and I gained materially as well. I thought they loved me. But it is always lonely at the top. I craved for a true friendship; at the same time, my ego came in my way to a friendship with a lesser mortal. I thought I was sitting on the chair, but in effect, it was the chair that used to sit on me." Aniruddha paused and coughed. Then he continued again. "I learnt it the hard way. After retirement, I had to stand in the queue for gas cylinder, to get milk and nearly at all the offices and stores; including our own Coal India office. It took time for me to realise that I am no more important. Moreover, other retired people have got their own association and circles. They associate with me, but don't gel with me. It is all my fault. I was arrogant, high-headed and what not! My house is near to this place only. As I was having an evening stroll, I saw your name on the board outside your clinic and thought to have a chat with you. I have got my regular physician who looks after my blood pressure and diabetes. But since I have enlisted myself as a patient, you might as well check my blood pressure." Aniruddha advanced his arm on the table and smiled again.

"With pleasure, sir." Probir started wrapping the BP cuff on Aniruddha's arm. "It is slightly on the higher side, sir. It can easily be controlled with a bit of adjustment in drugs," he said after the measurement was completed.

"May be that is because of the momentary excitement I had while talking to you," said Aniruddha, "but forget about BP. How is your wife?"

"She is reasonably fine with minor age related problems."

"Charu, my wife will be pleased to know of her. They were quite friendly, I believe." Aniruddha smiled again.

"I believe so as well, sir." Probir was not so sure anyway.

Suddenly Aniruddha clasped Probir's hand. "Will you drop that 'sir' now? Can't you call me *dada* or something less sinister?" There was a glitter in his eyes. They were pleading.

Probir felt for the man. He smiled and took both Aniruddha's hands into his. "Why, of course Aniruddha-da. And say my regards to *boudi*."

Aniruddha smiled from ear-to-ear. "That won't do. I know my wife well. Do you think she would leave me alone after she comes to know that I met you? Your elder brother is inviting you couple to have lunch with us next Sunday. We will spend the entire day together; we will sing, chat and remember our old time. You are free to abuse me as much as you like." He burst out laughing. Then he wrote his address in a slip and handed it over to Probir.

"We have an invitation for lunch next Sunday." Probir announced as he entered his flat.

"It must be from Mr. Nair!" Bidisha was excited. The Nair family is very close to them.

"No, it is from someone else," Probir said with a quizzical glance. "It is a sort of return invitation, one should say. You have to wait till Sunday to come to know who it is from. All I can say at present is you know them pretty well."

"You and your suspense!" Bidisha is well acquainted with the queer way in which her husband behaves at times. All she can do is to wait.

ZOJI-LA

The Toyota Innova rolled smoothly uphill on serpentine road on its way from Sonamarg to Kargil. Abhijit and his family had just had breakfast at Sonamarg. Shreya and Rintu, the children had a ride on pony and they were discussing the same animatedly. Kirpal Singh, the young driver was a man of few words and he kept a strong vigil on the road with his hands steady on the steering wheel. This was considered to be one of the deadliest of Indian highways. They were on national highway 1D, curving its way through the Himalayan ranges. At present they were at a height of approximately 7,000 feet above the sea level and were surrounded by mountain ranges with no blade of grass on them. The colour varied from grey to brick-red to even black. There were occasional patches of snow in some distant mountains. These kinds of mountains are rare in the geographical region the passengers of the car belong to. Abhijit is a specialist in internal medicine in one of the Bhubaneswar hospitals. It is difficult for him to get a leave for a long period because of his busy schedule. But when the invitation to visit Leh came from none other than Brigadier Chandrachud Gehlot, Annapurna, Abhijit's wife was bent on going on with this outing. She had many reasons to press for it. Suprava, Chandrachud's wife had been one of the best friends of Annapurna and it was learnt that she was there at Leh visiting her husband as summers are open for the families to visit the army officers. Then in this time of May, Shreya and Rintu are free with their summer vacation on. Rintu has just passed class 10th and his elder sister Shreya has passed 11th. Next year Shreya will get too busy with her school leaving exam. Finally Abhijit had to relent. He was excited of the visit too. Abhijit was posted at Kargil long back as a young Captain. He was with the 9 Garhwal Rifles that time as a Regimental Medical Officer (RMO). Chandrachud was also a Captain as an Infantry officer those days. They used to have fun together then. Both of them got married about the same time. Lot of time has elapsed since then. Abhijit was transferred from infantry and did his post graduation to be posted subsequently to medical units or military hospitals. After completion of commission he left army and joined a hospital in his home town of Bhubaneswar. That was nine years' back. His children were born a little later than it should have been; there was some medical problem with Annapurna. Chandrachud, on his part had continued with his army job and was now commanding a brigade at Leh. His only son had just entered the army as a Lieutenant. They had been in touch throughout these years. It should be fun to relive those nostalgic moments once again. Moreover, at midway past fifty there is a new set of insecurity which creeps up. *Let's meet when time permits. You never know when you have to repent for not doing so.* By God's grace at fifty five Abhijit had a sound health. Annapurna was comparatively fragile in spite of being in her early fifties only. She had diabetes right from the age of forty and recently she has come up with deficiency of thyroid hormone. She was under the guidance of her husband only and maintained a reasonable health.

"Look, isn't it beautiful?" Annapurna pointed at the silky river flowing through the valley which looked far down. There were flocks of lambs grazing on the bank of the river. From the car the river looked like a ribbon of silk. Annapurna was well clad in her warm clothing inclusive of long coat and gloves. She did not want to take any chance. For the others, pullovers or jackets sufficed.

"What's the name of the river?" Rintu asked.

"It is the Sindhu. It flows to Pakistan." Shreya is an avid net user and generally refers to the Wikipedia before visiting a new place. It comes handy to establish her supremacy over her brother.

"You should have seen the river in January or February. It does not flow that time." Abhijit told.

"What for?" Shreya looked surprised.

"Because the water freezes, you moron." Rintu laughed aloud. It was his turn to be one up over his elder sister.

"Yes, the surface of the river freezes into beautiful wavy forms. It looks like a masterpiece by some great artist," said Abhijit.

"How long it takes to reach Zoji-La?" Shreya asked, "It should not be far away from Sonamarg."

"It is only nine km from Sonamarg; but in hills it takes at least half an hour to reach there." The information came from Kirpal Singh this time. All of them had developed a liking for this young Sikh lad in these two days. They had hired the vehicle from a known travel agency at Jammu. They were informed that in spite of his young age of nineteen he is one of the best in the business. And that showed. He drove well and behaved well. Rintu, who had been taking the photographs with a small camera, had taken numerous photographs of Kirpal in addition to the routine landscape snaps.

"What is BRO?" Rintu asked as he took a snap of one of the signposts.

"It is the Border Roads Organisation, the Beacon unit of BRO looks after the maintenance and clearance of this road." Shreya was happy to share her knowledge.

"Beacon is the light that flickers on the top of the VIP cars, isn't it?" Rintu had previously heard of beacons.

"You can apply the same here as well. Beacon is the bright light of the BRO over here. The BRO is an engineer unit of the army itself. The Border roads people stay here throughout the year and they do a splendid job," said Abhijit, "but sometime they also can't help and the process takes days together."

"I hope we are not stuck in the road due to some mishap." Annapurna was scared.

Abhijit looked at the clear sky where some unknown birds were trying to flirt with the isolated patches of white cloud. He smiled. "It doesn't look probable this season. But with Himalayan Mountains you never know."

The vehicles on the highway had come to a very slow motion as they moved in a line. The depth of the mountain passes from the side looked eerie. "We are approaching Zoji-La," Kirpal announced. "It is little more than eleven and half thousand feet above the sea level."

"11,575 as far as I can recollect," Shreya added to the information. A touch of smugness was obvious in her voice. The vehicle moved to a place where the road was bordered by greyish black naked hills on both the sides. A signpost by the Border Roads showed 'Zoji-La' with height marked 11649 feet above the sea level. The vehicle stopped for a few minutes. Rintu's camera came promptly into action. A villager went past with a herd of mules. Shreya kept frowning at the signpost.

"See, your Wikipedia is not true always." Rintu winked at Shreya with a diabolic smile on his face. He was finished with his photography for the time being.

Shreya threw a deadly glance on Rintu. "It's only a few feet higher," she grumbled.

"We are going to encounter an even higher pass tomorrow. It will be on our way from Kargil to Leh. It is called 'Fotu-La.' It is more than 13,000 feet." Abhijit made an effort to end the controversy. "However, Zoji-La is the more famous of the two for its historic importance. It was captured by the Pakistani forces in 1948, only to be captured back by the Indian forces in an operation called 'operation bison.'"

The vehicles had started moving again. Annapurna had utilised the break to sip coffee from the flask she was carrying with her. She was getting increasingly scared of the road. At places the steep downward slope in the side of the road led miles underneath. Not that she was new to this road. But then she was young and newly married. Everything in life had a positive meaning then. She was at least glad that the Zoji-La was gone.

"It was at this very Zoji-La I came for a rescue work as a young captain." Abhijit said.

"You mentioned about it once," said Annapurna. But that was only a passing remark. She wanted to know the details but Abhijit did not go into it.

"Why, were you not married that time, mom?" asked Shreya.

"It was just before our marriage. In any case, it is a field station and most of the time family is not allowed here. Your mom is not aware of many of the adventures of my life over here." Abhijit smiled and glanced at Annapurna. "But the Zoji-La thing was one to remember. It is here I came across one of the bravest persons I ever met."

Rintu and Shreya realised that there was a story in the offing. They huddled around there mother in the back seat. Army personnel, specially the retired ones are full of stories. But their father was an aberration. He didn't like to talk much about himself and even if he liked, there was hardly any time for Dr. (Col) Abhijit Mishra, one of the busiest physicians at Bhubaneswar.

"It was the end of January; the year was—let me remember__ 1987. My application for one month of annual leave had been granted and I was to leave station in a day or two. I was generally in a buoyant mood and more so as I was going to get married in that leave." There was a combined 'wow' from the children. Abhijit ignored it and continued. "It was then Col. Sharma, our the then commanding officer called me. 'Doctor,' he said, 'I'm afraid you have to move urgently to the Zoji-La. There has been a road block due to heavy snowfall and some civilians, including ladies and children have got stuck over there. As per the Border Roads sources, it is unlikely to open before a fortnight. We are sending a rescue team over there. Captain Gehlot (the same Chandrachud we are visiting) will be in charge of the rescue with Subedar Nanak Ram and Sep. Chhabilal to help him. You will look after the medical part and will be assisted by your nursing assistant Gajraj. You have only fifteen minutes to pack up your requirements. In case of any shortage of medicines you can take help from nearby 121 Field Ambulance. The helicopter will be arriving any moment from now.'

My heart sank. An order stays an order in army. But why *me*? Col. Sharma possibly read my mind. 'Capt. Mishra, I'm not heartless either. It will be good for you. After the rescue work is over; in my estimate that should take a couple of days, you can move by the rescue helicopter itself to Jammu. That will save you time. Your leave stays. Get ready fast.' Then he winked at me with a smile. 'And wish you the best for your marriage.' I smiled and saluted him. 'I am on my way, sir.'"

"Did the Air Force pilots bring the helicopter there?" Rintu asked. He was always fascinated by happenings in the Armed Forces.

"No, it was the air-op section of the artillery. It had recently come into vogue. Army had its own pilots trained for this minor operations." Abhijit said.

"Minor operations!" Annapurna was a bit surprised.

Abhijit smiled. "By armed forces' standard it was a minor operation only. The artillery pilots brought a Chetak helicopter and all the five of us boarded on it with our equipments and ration."

"How many persons a helicopter can carry?" Rintu asked.

"Chetak helicopters can carry seven to eight persons. They are principally used for goods carrying. A Cheetah helicopter is smaller. It can carry two to three persons other than the two pilots. I haven't seen any other helicopter and I don't know much about that either," Abhijit confessed.

"You would better listen to what happened then," commented Shreya.

"The Chetak was landed in a relatively clear place. There was a chaos going on over there. Around 100 people had got stuck at the Zoji-La. They flocked around the helicopter to be rescued. Everyone wanted to go first." Abhijit resumed. "Chandrachud Gehlot controlled the situation somehow while I took stock of the casualties. An old man had already died of HAPO."

"What is HAPO?" Interrupted Shreya.

"It is a lung disorder of the high altitude. It is called High Altitude Pulmonary Oedema. Death is almost instantaneous. Others suffered from various degree of hypothermia, frost bite and hunger related problems. No wonder there; they were stuck in the hostile conditions for more than two days. The entire pass was engulfed in snow, the temperature being 20 to 30 degree subzero. They were more panic stricken than diseased. But it was surprising to notice that there was only one death so far. I suspected more deaths under the circumstances. It was learnt from the people over there that this was possible because of one person, a truck driver. His name was Pushpinder Singh Sodhi; I still remember his name. I looked at the man. A stout Sikh of about 35. He had a perpetual smile on his whiskered face. I learnt from the others that he and his assistant, a young boy had arranged for the firewood from the villages walking long distance in the snow, he cooked food for the people and kept their moral high during this period. Of course the others helped, but they were concerned more about their own folk than anybody else.

I was impressed by the man. 'You did a great job. But tell me how did you manage to feed so many people for two days?' The man laughed. 'Let grace be to the Almighty,' he said, 'the ration was there in the very truck I was driving. I am coming from Jammu and was carrying gunny bags of potato and onion in my truck to be carried to Srinagar market. For our convenience we keep some condiments in our trucks. I borrowed some condiments from other people as well. Utensils are there with me. We are surviving on a diet of onion and potato. So where is the problem Sahib?' indeed there is no problem when you are resolute to do something as great as that. But as I started to examine the persons I found that the condition of this Pushpinder Singh was the worst of them all. His right leg was bad with frost bite. However, his assistant was in a sound health. The reason was revealed by the boy himself. 'Pra-ji (elder brother) did not allow me much to roam around in the snow.' And this was justified by Pushpinder. 'How could I?' He said, 'It was I who promised his father that no harm will be done to him as long as I am there. My body is my own property; I can do whatever I like with that. But how can I push him into trouble. I hit him, I abuse him alright; but that is a different thing altogether. Don't you agree with me Sahib?' I was yet to a see man like this.

I informed him that he was to be evacuated to Jammu by the first sortie itself and that his right foot was in such a bad shape that it might have to be amputated in case of a delay. He objected vehemently. 'What are you talking of? Leave these people and go away? I can be of help if I stay back with you. You are talking of one leg. I don't mind sacrificing both the legs. I am a tiger and the tiger will go the last.' He twirled his huge moustaches."

"But won't you call it rather foolish than an act of bravery? He did a good job alright; but now since the Army was already there, there was no point in staying back." Annapurna tried to analyse the situation of Pushpinder.

"You may say so; but some people are that way," Abhijit said, "moreover, Army is not the ultimate solution to everything. The weather could have gone worse, leading to stoppage of evacuation by the pilots. In that case all would have got stuck for more time. They are the regular drivers in that area having a fair knowledge of the surroundings. They always come handy in such circumstances. Moreover, look at the great heart of his and his willingness to serve! I will still call it an act of rare bravery." He became silent for some time.

"What happened then dad?" Shreya asked.

"He stayed back with us helping us in the rescue work. 'The first person to be rescued is my *bitiya rani.*' Pushpinder came with this claim keeping his smile on before the first sortie was ready to leave for Jammu. 'Did you bring your daughter along with you?' Chandrachud asked. 'I didn't bring her alright, but she is a daughter to me all the same.' Before we could further question her, the driver called us to his truck. It was a well decorated truck like most others in the region. To our utter surprise there was a girl of about 18 sitting there with a very small infant stuck to her breast. 'She had given birth to a baby girl last night only' announced Pushpinder."

"A girl born at Zoji-La! Wonderful." Shreya clapped her hand in excitement.

Abhijit forced out a wry smile. "That was about the only wonderful thing. The rest of her story was sad. We learnt that she was from a village near Udhampur. She got friendly with a boy who had come to visit his uncle's place in the village from Srinagar. The boy promised to marry this girl and she got pregnant sometimes after that. The boy went back to Srinagar with the promise that he would come back soon with the permission of his parents and marry the girl. But he never came back. In due time her pregnancy was disclosed and she became a subject of abuse in the entire village. Her parents advised her to abort the child but she did not give up. At last she became desperate and left the village with a scant amount of money for Srinagar. She was travelling along with some other villagers in a van when she had labour pain. Last night the child was born with the help of some elderly ladies under the arrangements of Pushpinder. Pushpinder calls her his daughter since last night and made all the arrangements for the girl and the baby daughter in the cabin of the truck."

"Goodness gracious!" Annapurna sighed.

"We made sure that the girl along with her baby was sent by the first flight itself. The persons were sent as per priority. There was no serious casualty as such. Yet it took us about three days to send all the persons to Jammu as the helicopter could carry only five people in one flight." Abhijit was about to make a conclusion.

"When did Pushpinder go?" Rintu asked.

"He was true to his word. He went with the last sortie of evacuation." Abhijit said. "And it took me two further days to get out of the place. The five of us had to wait for two days as the weather got too bad for helicopters to fly. The four other Army personnel were taken back to Kargil and I was flown to Jammu as a special case."

"And did you reach for your marriage in time?" Shreya was anxious to know.

"Yes, I did. Didn't I Anu?" Abhijit looked affectionately at his wife. "But before leaving Jammu I made it a point to visit the medical college hospital over there."

"To meet Pushpinder Singh?" Annapurna tried to anticipate.

"Yes, the intention was basically to meet Pushpinder, but there I saw the girl with her baby as well. They were doing fine."

"And what happened to Pushpinder?" Annapurna asked impatiently.

"His right leg was amputated just below the knee." Abhijit told in a grim voice. "His wife was there beside him. She was sobbing. But Pushpinder seemed to be in the best of his spirit. 'Doctor Sahib, I'm happy that I could help some people in their need. I could have lost my leg in some other mishap as well; but the Almighty has given me a chance to prove my worth. I must thank Him.' I was overwhelmed. I said the same to his wife. 'You must be proud of your husband. Such a great job he has done. I'll see if there is a provision for Government finance in such cases,' I said.

'We don't need any assistance from the government. I have a small agricultural plot at my Punjab village and we will shift over there. That will help us to take care of our basic needs. But can you help us on one account?' Pushpinder said. I asked what I could do for him. 'We are married since nine years and we don't have a child of our own yet. I think there is a medical problem with either of us. Can you tell us a way we could possibly overcome it?' That was the first time I saw tear in his eyes. They were simple folks and unaware of the nuances of medical system. I told them that I will tell the concerned specialists to have a look at them before he was discharged. The couple was satisfied with that assurance only. Before leaving the hospital I made it a point to talk to the doctors of the concerned departments requesting them to have a look at their reproductive problem as well."

"Didn't you meet Pushpinder afterwards?" Rintu asked.

"Never. But he will be in my memory forever." Abhijit concealed a sigh.

"I wonder if the couple were blessed with a child later on. With all his good deeds God is sure to be kind on him." Annapurna wished the couple with all her heart.

"The fact is, God was kind on Pushpinder and his wife. They were blessed with a boy soon after that Zoji-La episode." Kirpal Singh, the driver spoke out after few minutes of silence had prevailed.

"How do *you* know it?" Abhijit was surprised.

"I am in the best position to know it;" smiled Kirpal, "I *am* the son of Pushpinder Singh Sodhi."

There was an overwhelming astonishment in the vehicle. No one had ever come across such a coincidence; not even in their dreams. Sometimes the facts are stranger than fiction, as they say it.

"Where is Pushpinder now-a-days?" Abhijit asked as he came to terms with his excitement.

"Papa is at Vilayat Kalan, our ancestral village at Punjab."

"Who else do stay there with him?" Abhijit asked.

"Only he and my mother. Zoji didi visits them often as she is married to a man in a nearby village only." Kirpal encountered a hairpin bend with élan.

"Who is Zoji didi?" Annapurna wondered.

Kirpal smiled again. "She is the child born at Zoji-La that day. My father only christened her so. She and her mother were taken to our village by my parents as the lady was refused to be accepted by her family any more. My mother told me everything when I grew up. Zoji didi's mother's name is Salma. They became our family members."

"But why doesn't Salma stay with your parents now?" Inquired Abhijit.

"Because she had committed suicide two years after she came to our village. It seems she had gone to Srinagar afterwards in search of Zoji didi's father, only to find out that the man was married long before he met Salma. How she committed suicide was not clear; but my father got a letter written by her from Srinagar describing everything. He received the mutilated body from police few days after that."

The Innova proceeded with the passengers in a complete state of silence. The milestone on the road showed Drass to be 10 km ahead. Shreya had a plan that she would inform Drass to be the second coldest human habitat on the Earth. But she forgot conveniently.

ZOMBIE

'Bizarre' should be the word closest enough; thought Vipul Tyagi. He could not think of a better word to describe the goings on of this organisation. 15 years of service as an engineer in the Coal India Limited, which he has done with utmost sincerity and now see where you are dumped! To the VTC, or the Vocational Training Centre, of all the places! Vipul Tyagi is efficient, has a degree from a reputed institute like the ISM Dhanbad. He has worked day in and day out to increase the production of his Amlai Open Cast Mines (AOCM) in the SECL, South Eastern Coalfields Limited. He was elevated to the post of Manager by dint of his ability about two years back when he was thirty-five and was generally seen as a prospective Chief General Manger in making. This was the time he had an exchange of words with his Sub Area Manager, his immediate boss. The matter in question was straightforward. There is a commission offered by the private coal buyers, which is proportionate to the number of trucks loaded by them. This is termed as road-sell. The total amount accumulates to a huge sum, which is distributed amongst different officers starting from the managers to the CGM at the top, keeping the seniority of the beneficiaries in mind. This has been the norm and maintaining a knowledgeable silence on this matter is the unwritten rule in the coal circle. That is the reason most managers are elated on promotion to that post. However, Vipul begged to differ. He wanted to keep his hands clean. He knew that he could not change the system, yet he did not want to be a part of it. He knew that if he could climb the top of the ladder, maybe he could do something about the menace. He told his SAM in no uncertain terms that he would not be a part of the beneficiaries of the road-sell and at the same time, he made it clear that he would not prove to be a hindrance to any such practice either. The Sub Area Manager was wise enough to understand that the 'vicious' thought process of his Manager did not augur well for the 'chain of healthy events' and made a quick recommendation for the transfer of Vipul Tyagi. He was transferred equally quickly to VTC as an in-charge, which is considered as an 'inert' post. Vipul's peers thought it to be the right thing to do for his outlandish ideology, the blame of which is generally attributed to his father; known to be a righteous man. That is how he landed up in the VTC about one and a half year back. However, he did not mind. He started the process of setting things right at the VTC. As a matter of fact, there were so many things that were to be set right. To start with, it was his own subordinate officer, Mr. Hiteshwar Gogoi, who had a habit of turning up late on some pretext or other. Even if he did, he would not prepare the note-sheets, not arrange for the stationeries and so on. This was, more or less the state of affair of the *babus* or the clerks. They hated to move from one table to other; let aside doing the writing and typing job. The lower level staffs and the daily wage staffs were the worst of the lot. They used to come once in three days and expected their attendance to be in place on a regular basis. In lieu, they did occasional private services to the *babus*. Vipul proved to be a hindrance to this symbiotic relationship in the office. Within a span of few weeks, he changed the face of a sluggish VTC. He has a domineering personality behind the sharp cut amiable features. He imposed regulations, used his vocal cords and used his charms to motivate the staffs at VTC and was successful to a great extent. Not that anyone gave any credit to him; but he liked order in his life and was satisfied with himself.

It was as good, or as bad a morning like any other; the only exception being it felt stuffy. Vipul pulled the chair in his office and sat down. The fan was running in full speed. He had applied for an air-conditioner to be fitted in the room. The decision was pending. The month of September is not that hot either; especially in this part of Madhya Pradesh. It rained in abundance for last few days. Now there was no rain and neither the winter had set in. Vipul yawned. He did not sleep well at night. There was no particular reason for the same; but it happens some time. For most of the year, he has to stay alone in his company quarter. His wife Sagarika stays at Dhanbad with their only daughter Lipi who is a student of standard four. Sagarika stayed with her husband during the initial few years of their marriage. She is townsfolk and gradually she discovered the fact that it was not possible for her to remain in the small time colliery place for long. There was no shopping mall, no decent theatre, not even a good coffee house! She did not develop a liking for the ladies around either. They seemed so naive; always talking about the mining circle and about how smart their husbands were. Above all, she missed her parents. Her in laws are from a village in UP and they pride themselves as farmers. She never had much regard for them and visited them only about two to three times in all the ten years of their marriage. In contrast, both her own parents are of a suave background. They were both teaching staffs in the same government college, with father having retired a year back. Therefore, initially on the pretext of feeling home sick she left for Dhanbad and stayed back for months' together. Later on, it became even easier. Lipi, their daughter became of a school going age and Sagarika did not consider the place worth admitting her bright child into a school where her career would be at stake. What better place can be there for her child than Dhanbad where two full-fledged professors are there at home to guide her? Even if there was a difference of opinion on this issue (like many other issues) with her husband, it was she, who won the argument. She nearly always did so. In case the logic did not go her way, she would be throwing tantrums and would pass select abuses aimed at nearly one and all of her in-laws' family. Vipul had always been afraid of meanness and he kept quiet. Not that he had irresistible moments of desire to slap his wife hard on her face; but that would be a barbarian act. He still remembers his mother saying after his marriage: "She is *your* wife and will remain to be so till she is alive. You have to adjust whatever the situation is; even at the cost of the happiness of us. She is your responsibility from now onwards."

Vipul has kept the promise made to his mother. In spite of strong desire, he could never hit his *responsibility* on her face. Sagarika has remained a visitor during the school holidays of Lipi. Vipul misses Lipi more than he misses his wife. The evenings feel forlorn. It was easy for him to take to alcohol under the circumstances; but he took to books. He reads on various subjects in addition to mining to keep himself busy. A young boy called Akhilesh from his villages stays fulltime with him. Akhilesh cooks the food and does the errands.

A cup of tea can be refreshing, thought Vipul. He pressed the bell placed on his table. Shobha entered the room. Shobha is one of the two female employees of the centre. The other one is Trisha. Both are in the post of General Mazdoor; the lowest rank in the coal belt, and they were appointed about a couple of years' back on compassionate ground following their husbands' death. This is a favour done to the persons who die while in service. The next of kin gets a job in his place. In case they are women; as is usually the case, they are given a easier place like the VT centre. Shobha and Trisha both were in their early thirties. Shobha's husband died of some cancer of abdomen whereas that of Trisha died in an accident. As neither of them cleared the 10th standard exams, they were given the post of General Mazdoor only. Out of them, Trisha studied up to class eight and she could understand a bit of English as well. That is why she has been given the duty of attendant to the in-charge officer Vipul. Shobha being illiterate does the general errand duties of the office. Gossipmongers attribute the allotment of duties to the better looks of Trisha; but Vipul remains unperturbed by the same, as he knows this to be far from the truth.

"Where is Trisha?" Asked Vipul.

"She hasn't turned up yet, sir." Shobha answered.

"Get me a cup of tea," said Vipul, "and ask Trisha to report to me before she signs the attendance register."

Shobha left. 8.30 AM is the latest by what a person can sign his or her attendance. It was a rule made by Vipul. It was 9.00 AM already. *Trisha has to be marked absent,* thought Vipul. He was engaged in his daily work.

It was at 10 in the morning Trisha reported to the office of Vipul.

"I'm sorry sir. There were a lot of jobs to be done at home." Trisha looked at the floor.

"I run an office Trisha. Everybody here, including me, has to abide by the rules. You would do better to take a casual leave for today." Vipul felt bad for the woman. He knew it must be difficult for a lone woman to run the household as well as do the jobs in the office. She has two kids to look after in the house. But he could not bend the rule under any circumstance.

"It will not be repeated henceforth sir, I promise you." Trisha tried a last ditch effort without much hope. She knew her boss well.

"I'm sorry, I can't do anything here. Either you put up an application of leave or I mark you absent." Vipul turned his eyes on the files on his table.

Trisha went back. She was not left with any CL this year. She was marked absent for the day. However, she stayed back in the office with the hope that things might be corrected at the end of the month when the attendance register goes to the finance office.

As she reflected back on the cause of her delay, she found it was not her fault altogether. It was mostly because of Arun Sharma, who came to her quarter, as she was getting ready for the office. Arun Sharma is a senior clerk in the Area Head Quarter. He was a friend to her deceased husband. Ever since the death of her husband, Arun has come to be of help in many ways. Apart from bringing out her dues from the office, he had instigated Trisha in filing a case against the car driver who hit her husband. After a trial of about one and half years, the court gave a verdict in her favour. She received Rs. 3 lakh as compensation from the owner of the car. In spite of these favours, Trisha did not like Arun Sharma much. He was a person always running after money. At forty-six, he had five children including two girls who were not so good looking. Not surprising, given his own vulture like features and a not so attractive wife of his. As per the norms, he has to arrange for quite an amount as a dowry for his daughters. Therefore, his efforts of helping Trisha out were not entirely selfless. He takes a cut in all the benefits Trisha gets. Out of the three lakhs Trisha got, he had taken a clean 50%, which included the incidental expenses of the trial. Trisha did not complain. She would have got nothing if the case were not put up for trial at all. But these days another trouble is creeping up; he has started making passes at Trisha, which she has ignored so far. She was not sure how long she would be able to resist him. Today morning he came to ask Trisha to invest her money in some policy and this ate away the valuable time she has to be prepared for her duty.

The next day proved to be equally bad for Trisha. Arun came again, and at the same time. Arun chooses this time as both her children are away to school.

"So Trisha, what did you think of the proposal?" Arun said, exposing his betel stained teeth.

"Arun-*Bhayia*, it will take some time for me to think about your proposal. And there is no ready money in hand either." Trisha said as she entered the room. A pink towel was still wrapped on her long hair. She had just come out after bath.

Arun could not take his eyes away from Trisha. "Alright, the scheme can wait. But didn't I tell you before not to address me *Bhayia*?" There was a mischievous smile on his face bordering to ugliness. The thought of being a brother to Trisha was the last thing he relished.

"I don't think you will relish being called uncle or anything like that either," Trisha smiled. She did not want to be rude to this man. In spite of his evil intentions, he could show Trisha avenues of earning money. And she needed lot of it if she was to lead a decent life. "May be we could discuss the policies some other time. I will get late again today if we start discussion right now."

"What if you get late?" Arun looked surprised.

"I am not a Babu like you. Moreover, I have a strict boss who does not relent to any plea. Yesterday I was late and he asked me to give an application for casual leave that I did not have. So he marked me absent in the register. However, I did not give up and did stay back for the entire day with the hope that it would be adjusted later on. But I don't want a repetition of the episode today and I want to report in time." Trisha sounded anxious.

"That's why I call you naive," Arun gave a knowledgeable nod, "you have done duties for more than two years and yet you don't know the organisation is called 'Coal India.' Here people remain absent for days' together and are still marked present. You are only bothering about being late for a day or two! Do you think you are working in Europe or in a private organisation?"

"But my boss is a man for discipline. Neither he does anything wrong, nor does he allow to do others wrong. Why only me, everyone in our office comes in time."

"Oh, that Tyagi? He of course has that ghost of honesty on his shoulder. That is why he is posted in a rotten place like VTC. However, don't bother about him. He can be taken care of. What for are the trade unions after all? Don't you pay your subscriptions for the party?" Arun Sharma himself is one of the smaller office bearers of a party.

Of course she did. Not only to one party only, she paid subscriptions to three parties, however unwillingly. But she had her doubts what the parties would do in time of need. She got out of her house and Arun had to leave. Arun offered her a lift in his bike, which she politely refused.

However, she got late again. There was a delay in getting a hired auto rickshaw and the barrier at the railway crossing was closed. The coal bearing train moved painfully slow.

"I'm sorry Trisha. You have to be marked absent again today in case you are not left with any leave. You can go home. There is no point in staying back." Vipul Tyagi was as stern as ever.

"But sir, have I ever been late so long? Don't I do my duty with full integrity all the time?" Trisha was hurt by the way her boss dealt with her.

Vipul realised this. "See Trisha, what I said to you was not to hurt you. It is what I say to all if they are not in time. There is no doubt that you are sincere and you are possibly more punctual than anybody else is in this office. And I appreciate you for that. But that does not merit any special favour. If I want to run this organisation properly, I have to be fair. Don't you agree?"

That day Trisha did not stay back. She went back to her quarter. She switched on her TV set and started watching some serial. She could not watch TV for long. The incidence in the office kept creeping back to her mind. The more she thought the more she became animated towards Vipul Tyagi. *This fellow tries to impose himself on others. What is the use! Can you give any benefit to anybody? No. Then why to induct all this show of discipline? As far as giving Sunday and holiday benefits are concerned, that is restricted to the minimum. You want to be honest and upright; be so. There are so many departments in which they get a lot of benefits without having to do much. And look at us! All because of that Tyagi fellow.* Then her focus of thought shifted on Arun Sharma. That man is not good. But at least he had favoured her in getting a bit of extra bucks. *What have I got to do with the personal traits of a person?* She thought. *I have to see what benefit I get from a person. My children may be small now; but they will grow up and need higher education. Then I have to get my daughter married. I have to make a house of my own. There is very little chance that my husband's folks are going to help me since I am already in service. Well, let's see what happens.*

The end of the month did not augur well for Trisha. Her attendance remained unchanged as it reached the pay office. She called Arun Sharma.

"So you call yourself a trade union office bearer! Now let me see how you can help me out. I give my subscription regularly." Trisha was not in a benevolent mood.

"You don't worry. I'll talk to the concerned persons and the matter will be solved in no time." Arun sounded confident. A leader had a talk with Vipul Tyagi on this issue. Vipul did not relent. The leader talked about getting it done in lieu of some money. Vipul still did not relent. Finally, the leader talked about serious consequences to Vipul in case he did not change his attitude. Vipul showed the leader the door. Vipul was not afraid of these small fry leaders. He never does any wrong. The corrupt people have got their loopholes on which the union leaders thrive on. Why should he be afraid of them?

While the pay slip was given, Trisha saw to her dismay that she got two days' salary less. Arun Sharma knew this. He reported to Trisha before she could summon him.

"That Vipul Tyagi guy is an idiot. Well, that's the reason he is in the VTC in the first place. Otherwise, what prevented him from being a king as a colliery manager! I believe it is something to do with a defect in the upper chamber." Arun tapped his temple.

"Well, that does not solve my problem," said Trisha, who was not interested about the whereabouts of Vipul's brain, "tell me a way how to get out of this so that I can receive my entire months' pay. You know that I'm in shortage of money all the time. You and your leadership!"

Arun Sharma was offended. Trisha is good looking; she has a charm about her. Arun realised that if he wanted to win the heart of the woman, he had to pay for it. The best way to win her heart was to get her access to some money. She loved money. Well, he did not bother much about winning a heart. He wanted her body. He wanted to touch it, caress it without her objecting to the same. It was a difficult proposition. He thought hard. Then he had an idea.

"Do you want to earn some money? I can assure you it will be a big amount. But without your consent it can't be done."

"You sound a bit phoney to me. Let's hear the idea." Trisha remained non-committal.

"The idea is a bit out-of-box. But it can fetch money for sure." Arun still beat around the bush.

"Drop the preliminaries, will you?"

"Okay, listen to it. Put up a written complaint to the Sub Area Manager that the Tyagi chap wanted to have an undue affair with you. He wanted to close the door of his office and wanted to kiss you or anything to that effect. Since you are a modest lady and you refused the move, you objected to such a pass and as a result he had marked you absent for two days." Arun looked at Trisha sheepishly.

"You must have gone out of your mind. Do you know where I'm going to land up by such a complaint? I will be a laughing stock to everybody around." Trisha was vehement in her objection.

"Nothing of that sort. On the contrary, you will be the object of sympathy in everyone's eye. May be you will be honoured for your chastity. That is not the point. On that ground, I can frame up a case in the local police station and later on in the sessions court. We can claim an amount to the tune of nearly five lakhs. Even if it comes to nothing, we can claim a good amount for a peaceful settlement from Tyagi." Arun's evil brain was in full flow.

"No one is going to believe it." Trisha was not encouraged at all. "Vipul Tyagi has a clear and honest picture about him and they are going to believe that I am the person who is framing him. Moreover, how can I frame an innocent person like him? Will not the curse of God fall on me?"

Women can never change, thought Arun. *On one hand, they think of the virtues and vices and on the other, they have this unlimited greed for money.* "Well, the decision is on you. If you choose the path of virtue, the things remain unchanged and you loss two days' salary. If you go through a little bit of treachery then there are so many things to gain." He said aloud and winked at Trisha. "You think of it and we can talk about it later." Arun believed in letting the prey play a bit before it is caught. He could imagine his share of profit and went back in a buoyant mood.

Arun proved to be right. It was greed that took the upper hand as far as Trisha was concerned. Trisha thought over the matter at night. The more she thought about it the more she saw the point. Why should she think of saving Vipul? What good he did to her? Moreover, if she wanted to be well off, it has to be at the expense of somebody else. If that 'somebody' is Vipul, how does it matter? Arun Sharma made a visit the next day and a letter was drafted in Hindi. It was hand written. Trisha has a clear handwriting. It was addressed to the Sub Area Manager. It was clearly mentioned that Vipul Tyagi had been making obscene suggestions to Trisha for some time, which she ignored. On that eventful day, he asked Trisha to kiss him on his face right in his office, which she protested. The request was repeated the next day again and that made Trisha furious and resulted in hurling select abuses on Vipul. As a punishment, Vipul had marked her absent for those two days. A request was made to make a departmental inquiry into it and take proper measures for outrage of modesty of woman worker in working place. At the end, Trisha neatly signed it. She handed the letter over to Arun. Arun happily pocketed the letter. He thought that he was in possession of a time bomb.

"Now you see what I can do. We can be richer by a lot. You simply stick to what I keep saying." Arun was so elated that he kissed Trisha on her cheek. Trisha neither liked it nor objected to it.

Arun Sharma left Trisha's house. The first thing he did was to make a few copies of the letter. The next day he sent the original one by post to the SAM. A copy was sent to the Chief General Manager with the mark 'for info only.'

It was the ninth day of October, Tuesday, 11AM. Vipul Tyagi was making a training chart for elderly employees on lifestyle after retirement. The intercom rang on his table. It was from Dibakar Tripathi, the Sub Area Manager.

"Vipul, I would like to see you urgently in my office. It is urgent." The SAM ordered. It is the same SAM under whom he worked as a manager.

"I will be there within no time sir." Vipul hung up.

The SAM was alone in the office when Vipul reached. Dibakar simply handed over the complaint letter of Trisha to Vipul. Vipul's face reddened in anger as he went through the letter. With some effort, he controlled himself and gave the letter back. "What do you make of it?" He asked his superior with a stiff jaw line.

"Listen Vipul, I know that this is part of a conspiracy against you. I know you too well to believe in any such rubbish." Vipul did not find any trace of artificiality in Dibakar's voice. "May be you are too honest to be kept in the mines," Dibakar continued, "yet I have my deepest regards for you for the same. No question on your integrity. But what happened exactly?"

"Nothing serious. This lady came late on two consecutive days and I had to mark her absent since she was not left with any leave. That is a routine at our centre. True that a union leader came to plead her case; but I did not give any heed to it." Vipul was matter of fact in his manner, though still fuming.

"When are you going to learn Vipul? These union leaders are vicious creatures and they rule the industry to a lot extent. It must be his handiwork. You shouldn't have been adamant on such issues. But anyway, the arrow is out of the bow already and we have to find out a way to tackle it. The nature of complaint is serious as the complainant is a lady. So many strings can be attached to the thing; I hope you realise that."

Vipul nodded. "What surprises me sir, the lady so long seemed decent enough to me. I don't understand why she did put up such an allegation on me out of the blue." Vipul sounded puzzled.

Dibakar smiled. "That's why they tell, 'the fortune of a man and character of a woman—" He stopped suddenly finding that Vipul was in no mood for proverbs at that moment. "Well," he frowned, "I have kept the letter to myself and trying to keep it a secret; but I doubt how far these things can be kept quiet, especially when there is a copy of the letter to the CGM. It will be opened by his PA and then everyone will come to know of it."

"Public opinion is hardly of any concern to me sir; and you know that well enough. As long as I am in the right path, I can tackle all hurdles. Please don't worry about me." Vipul went out with his head held high. He went back to his office and asked for Trisha. She was not present in the VTC.

The apprehensions of Dibakar Tripathi came to be true. Everyone in the area knew the story by the end of the next day. The reactions varied widely. Some discarded and rubbished the allegation altogether. However, this number was limited to the well-wishers of Vipul and to those who knew him well. The maximum number however, was of the persons who showed sympathy to Vipul outwardly, but enjoyed inside about such a spicy event. Then there were few who kept saying openly, 'Rightly served. I always knew what a hypocrite he is.' Vipul kept doing his duty as before. All he wanted was to ask Trisha why she did it. Nevertheless, he did not get a chance. She had been absenting ever since she put up the complaint.

A departmental enquiry committee was set up comprising of two lady-officers and two male officers inclusive of the SAM. The enquiry was held soon after the complaint was made. The venue for the same was the VTC itself. Trisha was called to be interrogated, and so was Vipul. They were called in turns and never faced each other during the interrogation. The other staffs of the centre were also called as and when required.

After his interrogation was over, Vipul came out of the room and walked leisurely towards his office. That is when he saw Trisha going out of the centre. Arun Sharma was waiting for her with his bike in the porch. Vipul's first reaction was to ignore her. Then suddenly he changed his mind.

"Trisha, will you mind stopping for a minute?" He called aloud. Trisha stopped and looked towards the floor.

Vipul approached him. "Was this very much required, Trisha? Have you got any idea what turmoil I have to go through because of this irresponsible act of yours?"

Trisha did not answer. She kept twirling the corner of her sari on her finger. Arun Sharma shouted from the porch, "You don't have to answer anything to him. Come now, we'll have to leave." Trisha was perspiring. She left in haste. Hiteshwar Gogoi, the senior engineer under Vipul came forward. He had seen them from a distance.

"There is no point asking her any questions, sir. She is under the influence of that Arun Sharma, who is evil to the core." Gogoi looked at the two of them departing in Arun's bike.

"But how did he make her agree to write such a letter? Is she out of her senses?" It remained a puzzle to Vipul.

"Rumour goes that the two are having an affair. But my guess is, it has more to do with money than anything else."

Vipul realised that it was just the beginning of his misery.

The report of the enquiry committee was out within three days' time. They did not find any fault with Vipul. Neither his record, nor the circumstantial evidence suggested anything that could find him guilty. Vipul was given a clean chit and Trisha was reprimanded and she was transferred to a dispensary.

However, the matter was far from solved. Arun Sharma never gave up that easily.

"IPC 509 is easily applicable. With some effort, we can drag it to 354. That amounts to two years' imprisonment and fine, or fine only, or both." Durjan Thakur lifted his plump whiskered face from his book. His small eyes were twinkling behind the rectangular reading glasses. Durjan practices in the sessions court of Burhar, the nearest one in the area. Durjan is not the leading criminal lawyer, but he has a reputation for hooking some innocent person and he is a favourite with Arun Sharma. "354 pertains to use of force with a view to molestation, whereas 509 is applicable for simpler offences like making a meaningful gesture at a female and so on. As far as I can gather you are more interested in the compensation part of it. Am I right?" Questioned Durjan Thakur to Arun Sharma, who was sitting opposite to him on the other side of the table.

"Spot on, I should say," winked Arun, "make the compensation amount big Thakur-Sahib. Your end will be taken care of. I am not bothered which section of penal code you apply. Barring your professional fees, you get 10% of the compensation package. That's a deal."

Durjan was pleased. "You had been true to your words before. I will see what can be done at the best. But tell me; was there any advance from the officer concerned at all?"

"It is said that one must disclose everything to his doctor and lawyer," Arun bared his ugly teeth, "no, there was none whatsoever."

"So, it is a pure case of framing." Durjan smiled. "But tell me one thing; how did you make the female ready to write the letter? Having an affair?"

"I have affair with money only. If something comes in addition, I am not a saint to ignore that either." Arun laughed making a filthy noise. Even Durjan did not like the sound of the laughter.

The school holiday of Lipi, Vipul's daughter was about to begin. It was Dussehra and Diwali times. Sagarika had an option of choosing between going to Vipul at Amlai colliery or calling him to Dhanbad. She was contemplating on the correct option. If she were to visit Vipul, she would have to arrange for the railway tickets. It was evening and she thought of calling Vipul. It was then her cell phone rang. It was Vipul. She wondered whether something like telepathy existed at all.

"I was just planning to call you," Sagarika chirped.

"Good that I saved you money." Vipul gave a wry smile. "When is Lipi's school vacation starting?"

"It was about that only I wanted to take your opinion;" Sagarika used craft to put it up, "the vacation starts in a weeks' time. Can't you come for a few days to Dhanbad so that we stay here for the Dussehra festival? Mom and Dad also want to see you." There was a silence at the other end. Then she added hastily, "Of course we'll be back at Amlai for Diwali."

The momentary silence at the other end was not because of Vipul's aversion to Dhanbad; he was searching for the proper words to put up the recent developments to Sagarika.

"That should have been fine," he said, "but I don't think I can leave station at this time."

"It must be that production thing in the mines again," Sagarika forgot all her tact within a moment, "I'm fed up of your mines. Can't they spare you even on festivals?"

Vipul appeared cool at the other end. "You seem to forget that I am no more in the mines these days. I work at the VTC. It has nothing to do with production. I am about to face a trial in the local court of law."

"Oh God! What for?" Sagarika was anxious.

"I have been framed. My office peon Trisha has put up a complaint in the court that I tried to outrage her modesty in the office." Vipul put the facts plainly.

"Trisha!" Exclaimed Sagarika, "I met her once. She seemed dignified enough to me." She thought quietly for a moment. "And as far as I know you, I can't even imagine you doing such a thing. There must be someone else involved."

Vipul was relieved to hear that. He was not sure how his wife was going to take it. At times, she shows remarkable maturity. May be there is a feminine instinct which helps. "You are right. There is a clerk at the area office that is playing the game."

"Tell me more about it." Sagarika was all concentration.

"There is not much excepting it is an undue problem which I could do without. A departmental enquiry went in my favour. Then they put the case up in the local court. The local police summoned me once and our legal officer arranged a bail for me. Our department has made all the arrangements for me to fight the case. It is not much to worry about."

"Not much to worry about?" Shouted Sagarika, "Do you think the scandal will go unnoticed? Yours detractors, which are many, are going to make hay of the situation. Your career can be at stake."

"As long as I am in the right path I am not afraid of anyone. And with you on my side I can touch the sky; you know that Sagarika." The voice of Vipul was sublime.

"Yet I am afraid, Vipul. I will reach you as soon as possible. Take care till then."

"I love you."

"So do I."

If the incidence of Trisha Namdev, a General Mazdoor at VTC putting up an allegation of outrage of modesty against her departmental head Vipul Tyagi was known to a few in the colliery circle, Arun Sharma made it sure that everybody around, including folks outside the colliery came to know of it. He made the story public with full-page news published in the local newspaper. It was easy, considering the fact that the local news reporters do not give heed to things like integrity as long as it is in lieu of appropriate amount paid to them. Life became more difficult for Vipul. People met him with a mask of sympathy. "We know that it is not true. But how did it start exactly?" They would ask. Vipul had to say all about it. As soon as he was out of sight, the conversation used to take another turn.

"That woman is not good," someone would say, "may be she was trying to hook Vipul. His wife doesn't stay with him. He might have been fond of the feminine touch as well. One cannot deny she is good looking. It is possible that she was caught in the act and then put all the allegations on Vipul."

"She has hooked Arun Sharma as well. I heard it is all that Sharma's brainwork." Somebody else would say.

"That's why I am scared of all the female staffs in my office," a third person would interrupt, "whatever the age and however bad looking."

Everyone would laugh.

Nevertheless, it was not very funny for Sagarika who had arrived in the station in the mean time. "We must sue that newspaper and slap a defamation suit against that woman," she fumed.

The first hearing was fixed just before the Durga Puja. "The case does not have any standing." Pranab Dastidar, the law officer of CIL for Vipul was casual about it. Later on, you can drag the woman to the court on charge of defamation. Vipul kept quiet. He did not know much about the nuances of law. All he wanted to do was to get out of the mess. Arun Sharma was having a great time. He bragged about how he stood behind a widow at the time of her need. He was ready to tell all and sundry the tragic story of Trisha and he found many takers.

Trisha appeared on the day of first hearing. She avoided any look or eye contact with Vipul in the courtroom. Pranab Dastidar tried to cross question Trisha on the details of the incidence. "I have given the details in my complaint letter. I don't want to elaborate further in the court." She said. There was an objection from Durjan Thakur, Trisha's lawyer on the ground that it was too embarrassing for a lady to elaborate these things in front of the court. The objection was sustained. The complainant, however, gained on one point. They managed to produce one witness, Ram Swaroop, the local mail carrier, who gave a vivid description of how he had seen Vipul making obscene gestures to Trisha as he went to deliver a letter at Vipul's office on the 25th of September. On verification, it was confirmed that Vipul indeed received a registered letter on that day from the Mines' Safety Department. Durjan had gone through the homework meticulously! Cross-questioning of the mail carrier did not prove to be fruitful for Pranab. The man was trained and bribed well.

"Things are getting complicated. But don't worry. This is not out of our hands. I have to go more prepared the next hearing." Pranab assured Vipul as they came out of the sessions court. Needless to say, it did not do much to the confidence of Vipul.

"I'll go and talk to Trisha. Let's see how she faces me." Sagarika told after hearing the entire court process from Vipul at night. Vipul looked disturbed. Sagarika thought that she must do her part in the given scenario. "Do you know where she stays?"

"Her quarter is somewhere near the colliery railway crossing, I am not sure." Vipul told. "But there is no point in your going there. I talked to her once. She won't relent. Moreover, this will be another talking point to the people." Vipul was also afraid of the fact that Sagarika might loss her fragile temper and start a show off there.

"Don't you worry," Sagarika understood and even forced out a smile, "I will only try to pursue her to withdraw her complaint."

Vipul did not answer and started playing with Lipi. *Why should this sweet girl suffer because of her father's problems?* He thought.

Trisha was ready for her duty the next morning. There was still some time left before she could start. Sruti and Samrat, her daughter and son respectively, were having some dispute over a trifle. There vacation had started. She thought of scolding them. Then decided otherwise. She had a headache. She was not sleeping well since few days. She went towards the window for some fresh air. Then she saw the lady getting down from an auto rickshaw. The lady was smartly attired. She asked someone something. The man pointed his finger towards Trisha's house and she started walking towards it. Then Trisha realised. It was Vipul Tyagi's wife. She had seen her once. Trisha's heart gave a leap. She hastily closed the window, bolted the door, and kept quiet.

The doorbell rang. There was no answer from inside. The children jumped up to unbolt the door. Trisha indicated them the keep quiet.

"Open the door Trisha. I know you are there. I am Mrs. Tyagi." Sagarika's voice was steady, yet stern.

There was no reply.

"There is no use pretending that you can't listen to me. And you know why I am here." Sagarika did not loss her cool.

"Madam, I also know that you are there. I saw you coming. I don't want to talk to you." Trisha answered this time.

"Why not, Trisha? If you are not guilty, why are you afraid of facing me? If my husband is wrong, I believe you have every right to do whatever you are doing. But if he is not, then you must be doing it under some pressure from elsewhere. Can't you withdraw your complaint if he is not wrong?" Sagarika pleaded from outside.

"I have told whatever I had to. My lawyer will do the further talking. I do not want to answer any of your questions. Please go back."

Trisha thought Sagarika would retaliate. Instead, her voice was broken. "I am going back. I thought that as a woman you would understand my position and have sympathy on me. May be I was wrong in judging you. But remember, there is a Judge above all of us Who always does justice." Then she left.

Trisha sat quiet for some time and then in an impulse opened the door. She saw Sagarika catch an auto rickshaw. She was wiping her eyes with a hanky.

"Who was that woman Ma? Why didn't you allow her to get in?" Sruti looked surprised.

"None of your business. Go and play." Trisha told roughly.

Sagarika thought she would continue to be with her husband and see the end of this. School of Lipi could wait. However, that was not to be. Her father suffered a heart attack and she had to rush back to Dhanbad. The next hearing was fixed only a week after her departure. She left with a heavy heart.

Talking of hearts, that of Arun Sharma was going great guns. He kept in touch with Trisha on a regular basis. One evening, as he entered her house he saw both the children out of the house.

"Where are Sruti and Samrat?" He asked.

"They are out to attend a birthday party in the neighbourhood," she answered.

"Good that they are enjoying," Arun said buoyantly, "soon it will be our turn to rejoice. I think the compensation package is not far off. May be it will take two or three more hearings. Our counsel says we will get around four lakhs; all expense paid. That comes to around two lakhs to each of us. Durjan Thakur is a clever guy. How effectively he brought the mail carrier into fray! Now do you agree that my idea was brilliant? And you were not willing for it in the first place! That's why I say, as a team we can do wonders."

There was no reply from the other side. Trisha was not listening properly. She was thinking of the words from Sagarika. She mentioned something about the justice by God. Trisha was a god-fearing woman.

"Where are you lost Trisha?" Arun asked.

"Oh, it's nothing," she said, "how much did you say I will get?"

"We are to receive a little more than four lakhs," Arun sounded jubilant, "the incidental expenses will come to be, say about a lakh, and we are to receive two lakhs each. Even if the expenses come to be more than that, I will give it from my share. You are going to receive a cool two lakhs." *It is the time to show some benevolence,* thought Arun.

"That's a good amount," Trisha looked cheerful. She forgot about her conversation with Sagarika. Money is the elixir for so many worries!

"Well," began Arun somewhat hesitantly, "now that we are acting as a team for such a long time, won't you allow some personal intimacy as well?" He looked at Trisha. She was sitting on the couch with her head lowered down. Encouraged, he continued, "I know that socially it is not permissible, but the fact is that I have fallen in love with you, and you are aware of that. It is difficult for a widow to manage her living alone. Still I leave it to you. I don't want to do anything against your will." He looked hopefully at Trisha.

Trisha was still looking at the floor playing with the corner of her sari. Arun Sharma took it as a positive sign and embraced her. There was a sweat mixed odour of tobacco from Arun's body, which Trisha detested. But after all, it was a masculine touch after a long time. Her body relaxed. Arun kissed her on the lips. She responded and kissed back. Her body started feeling good and she held Arun tightly. They went to bed. Trisha switched off the light.

Next morning Trisha woke up with a headache. She was feeling bad for whatever happened last night. She thought she was going down an eternal gutter and there was no way out for her. First, she has framed an innocent man for doing the right thing; then she has teamed up with a filthy man for her materialistic benefit. *Then what is the use of worshipping so many idols and fearing God? I have committed a sin,* She thought.

"Ma, come and have a look at Samrat. He is not feeling well." Sruti came to Trisha's room.

"What happened to him?" Trisha asked.

"I don't know." Sruti went back.

Trisha called Samrat aloud as she reached the children's bed. He did not respond. He was shivering. She felt her son's chest with the back of her hand. He was running high temperature. She always kept some medicines as an emergency measure in a plastic box. She took out a tablet named Paracetamol and asked Samrat to swallow half of the tablet. Samrat swallowed the same with some difficulty. Soon after, he vomited out. He vomited couple of times more. Trisha decided that it was not the time to waste. "Sruti, call an auto rickshaw from the road. I have to take Samrat to the hospital," she told.

It was two hours after taking him to the hospital that the physician told her, "I am afraid he has got a cerebral form of malaria."

"How bad is that doctor?" She asked anxiously.

"It is pretty bad. He is not conscious now. I am trying my best. But nothing can be told with certainty till forty eight hours have passed." The doctor said.

Trisha was on the verge of tears. *It is all my fault,* she thought. *But O God! Why should this innocent suffer for her mother's sin? Do whatever You like to me; but spare the child.* She folded her hands and brought them to her forehead in prayer of the Omnipotent.

Arun Sharma came to the hospital on hearing the news. "We can shift him to a larger hospital with better facilities if you like. In any case, you should have given me the information." He complained.

"I can take care of him. You go and do your job." Trisha said rather curtly.

Arun was surprised and yet he did not mind. He was happy in a way that he was kept out of trouble's way. "Soon he is going to be alright. Give me a call if required." He left the hospital.

Sruti came for a while in the evening to relieve Trisha. Trisha took a bath at her quarter. She had half a mind to have a quick grab. But she could not have even a morsel of food. The helpless face of Samrat kept hovering over her eyes. There were numerous idols of gods and goddesses in her storeroom. She fell flat on her belly in front of the idols and started weeping; relentlessly. 'O God! Forgive me,' she kept saying.

Whether it was because of the earnest prayers of Trisha or because of the treating skills of the doctors, it was not clear; but Samrat started improving from the third day after his admission. He recovered full consciousness and soon was discharged from the hospital. He was well, though very weak. Arun Sharma expressed his happiness over recovery of Samrat and hoped that his relation with Trisha would improve. However, there was no visible sign of that. Then, he was a person who knew the worth of patience. He became busy with the preparation for the next hearing.

One evening he made a visit to Vipul Tyagi. Tyagi did not offer him a seat. Arun exposed his ugly teeth. "You are being cross with me for nothing, sir," he said, "I came to be of your help. If you pay some amount in cash, we will consider withdrawing the complaint against you. That will save you a lot of time and energy."

As for reply, Vipul Tyagi had simply driven Arun out and slammed the door behind him.

The condition of Sagarika's father had improved considerably. He had a mild cardiac attack and the doctor was of the opinion that he would not require any surgery; only some medication and precaution would do. Sagarika was relieved. She thought she would rejoin her husband and give him moral support. She even booked her railway ticket.

Sagarika was taking bath. She had a refreshing shower and was humming a tune while soaking her dry with a towel. Then she saw at her reflection at the large mirror in the bathroom. She was pleased. She had a good figure. She looked at her shapely breasts. She missed her husband. She fondly palpated her breasts. She felt a pang of pleasurable sensation. She kept palpating them for some more time. She felt her body relaxing. Then she stopped all of a sudden. *What is it! There is a hard lump at the upper and outer aspect of my right breast.* She started palpating her right breast with clinical precision. First with both hands, and then converging with two fingers. The lump felt hard beneath her fingers. It slipped to the sides escaping the fingers. She was alarmed. *Can it be a cancer? Well, it may be. How did I never sense it before?* All the relief and pleasure disappeared from her mind instantly. She came out of the bathroom quickly. She thought she would talk to her mother and then decided otherwise. *The first thing I will do tomorrow is to meet a surgeon,* she thought.

The date of the second hearing of Vipul tyagi's case fell soon after the Diwali. Vipul was summoned accordingly. He was a devastated by then. Reasons other than the case had more to do with it. The case was something, which he was capable to tackle. But something more ominous had happened in the meantime. It was only a couple of days back he had received the phone call from Sagarika. She was broken altogether. She was diagnosed to have breast cancer! The doctor there, after a barrage of tests, had confirmed the diagnosis. The worst was, it was in a late stage and the cancer had spread to several organs of her body. She had started taking chemotherapy and radiotherapy. The doctors had stated that it was beyond the scope of surgery. He thought of getting her treated at the best possible centre; but for this unnecessary trouble!

There were a considerable number of people that had gathered in the courtroom. There were the witnesses, some hangers on, some well-wishers, and some who were simply curious. Trisha was there to stress her point. Arun Sharma clang on to her like a perpetual leech. Vipul cast a disgusted look at Trisha. She lowered her head.

Questioning and cross-questioning of the witnesses continued. When it was the term of Vipul, he was asked to say the happenings of the day in question.

"Your honour!" He told, "I can't fathom out how a lady can stoop so low for some flimsy benefit."

"You are not here to preach moral lessons on women," interrupted Durjan Thakur, "answer only what is being asked of you."

"My lord," Trisha suddenly stood up from her position, "I want to speak a few words." Everyone looked at her in surprise.

"Please be quiet lady. Your turn will come." The judge struck his hammer on the table.

"Sir, it is urgent. May be I will not have the courage to speak it later." Trisha sounded desperate.

"Okay, come to the witness box and say whatever you have to." The judge said reluctantly.

"Your honour," Trisha said in a loud and clear voice, "I want to withdraw my complaint."

The hall came to a silence all of a sudden. There was a vacant look on Arun Sharma's face. He could not believe his ears.

"You mean to say you have agreed for an out of court settlement?" The judge wanted to get the point right.

"No sir. On the contrary, what I mean to say is, my complaint was absolutely baseless and I want to withdraw it with due apology to the court." Trisha was emphatic in her statement."

"Do you understand the implication, lady," the judge continued, "of such a confession? You can be punished for contempt of court, you can be dragged to the court again by the defendant on charges of defamation and in the least, your service record is going to suffer because of causing harassment to your superior officer."

"I am ready to face any consequence sir, it will be much less than what I have suffered already. At least I feel much relieved now that I have confessed the same." Trisha wiped the corner of her eyes with a small handkerchief.

"I have reasons to believe that you might have been instigated by someone to put up such a complaint." The judge continued his inquiry "Is it so?"

"Yes sir, it is true." Trisha said. Arun Sharma flinched and Durjan Thakur made sideways movements of his head. However, Trisha continued, "But that does not matter. It does not dilute my sin in any case. I am not going to name the person. As I have already told, I am ready to accept whatever punishment that is conferred on me." She lowered her head.

A faint hustle-bustle had started again in the courtroom. People were coming with various theories of their own. Vipul was surprised at the turn of events, but he looked oblivious to his surroundings. Arun and Durjan were discussing something animatedly. The judge left the court with announcement of lunch break. The verdict was to come out soon after the break.

The verdict was on the expected lines. Vipul Tyagi was acquitted of all charges with due honour and apology. Trisha had to sign a bond of apology and she was left with a reprimand only.

Three months had passed since then. Vipul was transferred to Dhanbad on compassionate ground soon after the verdict. Trisha was doing her duties of a peon at her dispensary, the new place of posting, sincerely. She was seldom undisciplined. However, there was a red ink entry in her career sheet. She did not mind that. She had learnt to live a plain and simple life. She had cut off all her connections with Arun Sharma. Arun was in search of a newer pasture.

One thing, a trivial one at that, kept pinching the conscience of Trisha. She wanted to talk to Vipul Tyagi and his wife in person once and ask for pardon. She could not do it as Vipul was transferred in a hurry.

Well, I can still ring them up and ask them to forgive me, she thought one day. With some effort, she gathered the cell number of Vipul and waited for evening to come when Vipul and his wife should be at home. At about eight thirty in the evening she rang the number up.

"Is it Mr. Tyagi?" Trisha asked hesitantly.

"That's right. May I know who is speaking?" The heavy, unmistakable voice of Vipul was there at the other end.

"Sir, it is Trisha, from Sohagpur area."

"Trisha! It is a surprise indeed. What can I do for you?" Vipul's voice was calm. Trisha could not make out whether he was still cross with her.

"Sir, I just rang up to know, can you, er— ever forgive me?" Then she went on to add in a hurry, "I wanted to ask for your pardon in person; but I didn't get a chance."

"Oh that! I was never cross with you; only I was a bit surprised. It is good that you have realised your mistake. Lead a life of honour and pride. Wish you all the best."

Trisha was relieved hugely, though she felt like sobbing. "Thank you so much sir," she said, "and one last request. Can I talk to madam once? I still repent the way I ignored her when she came to my house to talk to me. Can I say her 'sorry' for what I did?"

There was a long pause at the other end. "I am sorry to say that it is not possible. Sagarika has left for her heavenly abode about a month back." There was a deep sigh at the other end of the phone.

Trisha burst into an unexpected bout of cry. "Is it so sir? I know, it is all my fault. *I and only I* am to be blamed for her death. Never forgive me sir, never forgive me." Her voice choked in another bout of cry.

"Look Trisha, it is none of your fault. She had advanced stage of breast cancer and____" Vipul realised that no one was there at the other end of the phone.

A woman can stand all except the infidelity of her husband. Trisha thought when she went to bed that night. *Madam had her doubts in her mind. She thought there was some truth in my complaint. It is bad that she never realised what a god-like husband she had. But it is all because of me. She wanted to verify the facts from me. If only I could have told her the truth when she came here! Whatever the external cause may be, I am sure it is the mistrust in her husband that has eaten her up slowly but surely. I am filth. I do not deserve to live.* She had made up her mind. She woke up slowly. With a determined look on her face, she caught hold of a nylon rope. With the help of a chair placed over a table, she reached the ceiling fan and tied one end of the rope to the body of the fan. She fashioned the other end into a noose and stood on the chair. The only thing remained was to put her neck into the noose and kick the chair aside. It seemed easier than she thought!

"Ma, give me some water." It was Samrat whose voice came from the adjacent room. It was a weak voice, yet audible enough to reach Trisha's ear. Trisha jumped back on the ground and reached her son with a glass of water. Samrat drank the water and slept peacefully again. Nevertheless, to his mother, 'peace' remained an alien word.

I cannot shirk my responsibility. I cannot die, not now at least. What is the fault of Sruti and Samrat? Those tender lives will be spoilt once I die. I have to keep living for the time being. Yes, that is how I am going to pay for my sin. Trisha put the chair and table in their places after removing the rope from the fan. She kept awake for the rest of the night. Her eyes remained dry.

The story dates back three years from now. If you care to look at a woman going to dispensary number two at around eight in the morning every day, you will not like to have a second look at her. She looks ugly with her bony cheeks and sunken eyes. She barely breaths. She does not talk to anybody unless she has to, that too in monosyllables. She never smiles. For that matter, there is no play of emotion of any kind in her. If you care to go for inside information, then you come to know that she eats and drinks the bare minimum to keep herself alive. She takes care of her children and pays their school fees in her own, mechanical way. She never takes a leave. She never reacts to anything. She keeps moving like a machine. She is a zombie. Some say that she has lost her mental balance. Some others say it is a curse she is going through. Have a close look at her and you may find a semblance of the old self she was; she is our Trisha.

SULTAN SINGH

As a young Captain, in the capacity of Regimental Medical Officer of 11, Garhwal Rifles if I thought that my plight was over after a stint in Ladakh for one year, I was grossly mistaken. I opted to join the Army only little more than a year back and I was yet to know the way it functioned. Within a fortnight of coming back to Gwalior, the battalion was ordered to move to Kapurthala in Punjab. We were to be a part of the Operation Blue Star. The operation was started in response to some Sikh terrorist group who thought that annihilation of whatever came their way was the best way to start a revolution. But it was none of my concern. To me, there were outbursts of rages from various socio-cultural groups from time to time in past and the Government dealt with these in the best way it thought possible. The thing that concerned me was the troubles of moving back to yet another disturbed area leaving our peace station. But one cannot complain in Army. We did not either. It was July, in the year 1984. The Golden Temple at Amritsar had been a spot of tussle only a month back. Our battalion was sent as reinforcement to Kapurthala.

Once at Kapurthala, I discovered that the place was not bad whatsoever. It was a well developed Punjab town, like most in the state. The planning was not that good, however. The lanes were narrow and the buildings, mostly medium sized, were too close to each other for my liking. We were stationed in one of the local college buildings. The people in general were good natured, yet there was an amount of apprehension in the air. This was mainly because of the local administration had to take decisions in consultation with the Army. So much so that, the campus, in which we were station contained a section of top brasses from police and administrative services. That opened a newer vista for us, the Army personnel. Sometimes the local disputes were solved in presence of our Commanding Officer and some other times a Collector would join us for lunch and rue his decision of joining the elite Administrative Services. However, my job used to be of a little different nature. Most of the days, I would go to one of the nearby villages with my medical team and organise medical camps over there. I was generally accompanied by a team of CSD canteen led by a JCO who distributed canteen items to the villagers at a subsidised rate. In other words, I was a part of social service team of the Army which wanted to enhance the confidence of the people in Army in particular and the Government in general. My personal belief, however was, the people of Punjab had never lost their confidence in Army as one from almost each family in the state was there in the Armed Forces. That is apart from the point. They were generally happy to see our team in the villages and availed the opportunity to their best. The other thing I was supposed to do was to accompany the infantry men with an ambulance during the raids to the hideouts of the militants. Rarely there used to be encounters. Warnings from the Army personnel sufficed to bring them out from their sheds (often the gurdwaras served as the same). They were with their families in the hideouts and as soon as they came out, they were served food by the soldiers and medical benefits were extended by my team. There were numerous unique experiences that came my way during these excursions. But this story is not one to describe these. It is about someone who took undue benefit of the movement during those days.

His name was Sultan Singh. He was not a terrorist. He did not have an idealistic motto of any sort. He committed crimes for his own gain and let the blame fall upon the terrorist groups. There was almost no crime that he did not commit. The list envisaged burglary, murder, rape, extortion and so on. This was known to the local police. But they could hardly do a thing about it as he was influential. He had connections higher up in the political circle. To top it all, he was educated. He had a bachelor's degree in law and he used to practise in the local sessions court. In case I have not mentioned, Kapurthala used to be a sub divisional town in those days.

The local political circle being out of equation during the intrusion of the Army, the police top brass thought their chance to be ripe to settle their score with Sultan Singh. They requested the Army, or the CO of 11 Garh Rif Col. Rathi to help them out. Col. Rathi was more than willing. He sent a team under Capt. Chouhan to capture the culprit. Capt. Chouhan was a commando trained officer and he took four commando boys along with him which included a JCO, Subedar Ramkinker Joshi. The operation was done at night, at about 10 or so. Sultan Singh made a valiant attempt at fleeing from his home as he got the information beforehand. But it came to a naught in front of the commandos of the Army. He was caught and kept in the custody of the Army. Soon after the operation was over, Capt. Chouhan reached my room. He used to be one of my good friends as we were in the same age group. I was studying a book that time. Chouhan relaxed on a sofa in my room. There was no sign of exhaustion in his face. He was laughing. It seemed he had just returned from a stroll in the market.

"What is it Chou? You seem to enjoy your stay here. Have you got a letter from your fiancé?" I asked. Those days letter was the only form of communication one could have with their near and dears. Long distance phone calls were not much in vogue either.

"Well, last I had a letter from her was ten days' back. But this one is interesting Doc. I thought you will enjoy listening to it."

"Well, carry ahead." I slammed the book closed.

"It is about Sultan Singh." Chouhan was still laughing. I had knowledge that the Army was after Sultan and also that Chouhan was in-charge of the affair. I did not have any idea whether he was already caught and even if he was caught, what was funny about it. But Chouhan was a jolly boy and he could bring out a funny situation out of anything.

"Has he been caught already?" I asked.

"That was a foregone conclusion. With Commando Captain Pradeep Chouhan at the helm of affairs, you know." He pinched up the collar of his T-shirt. His well shaped hand showed a play of waves of muscles. Though he said this in the form of humour, I knew his capabilities well enough to put any doubt on that.

"You are an asset to the organisation," I smiled, "but what is so funny in it? Did you play one of your pranks on the poor chap?"

"Poor chap! Are you joking?" Chouhan stopped laughing. "He does not think himself anything below a superman. As soon as he knew we were approaching, he escaped through the backdoor of his house and got on the top of a nearby three storied building. We followed him. He started jumping away from the top of one building to the other. These buildings are quite adjacent to each other, you see. The scene was like that of a Hindi movie where the hero escapes that way. But he of course, had no idea about the Army men. We allowed him to play with us a little bit before we caught him. After his jumping over three consecutive buildings, we thought enough was enough. Sub Ramkinker wanted to be in the limelight and asked for my permission to catch him on his own. I permitted. The he ran in a gust like you have seen him in the *kabaddi* matches and caught up with Sultan in minutes. We reached soon after to see that the Sultan fellow was trying to fish out a pistol from his pocket. We simply stood aside to enjoy the fun. Ramkinker simply slapped him hard on the face and twisted his wrist hard enough to make the pistol fall from his hand. The scene that followed was cut out of pure movie staff."

"What happened?" I was into the thick of the thing.

"Sultan Singh suddenly straightened his chest and told, 'do you know who I am? I have got connections even at Delhi. You people are going to repent your actions.' To this Ramkinker twirled the end of his heavy moustaches and said, 'do you know who *I* am? In relation, I am your father and I *am* the Army.' You know what a movie buff this Ramkinker is and he did not spare this occasion of sticking a tagline on Sultan's face from the movie 'Shahenshah.' That of course was followed by another barrage of slaps from the Subedar. Sultan Singh must have had the shock of his life." Chouhan burst out laughing once more.

I started laughing as well. I also had seen the movie and it was one of the famous tagline of the great actor, Mr. Amitabh Bachchan.

"What happened afterwards?" I asked.

"Rest of the story is simple," Chouhan said, "Sultan Singh kept quiet ever since. He was handcuffed, tossed over into the jeep, and was brought here without any further disturbance. I think it was more to do with the filmy tagline of Ramkinker than his slaps."

"What did he look like?" I asked.

"He is handsome," Chouhan said with a chuckle, "could be passed for a movie hero, but for his crooked eyes."

"What is wrong with his eyes?"

"These are odd, with such a cold stare. He looks a born criminal. The man is evil to the core. Didn't somebody say, 'eyes are the mirror of mind?' He even used some English phrases, maybe to impress us."

"Seems an interesting character to me." I opined.

"May be he is too well connected to be in our captivity for long." This time Chouhan was serious.

"None of our business. This is the state of affairs with so many miscreants these days. Politician criminal nexus is heard of all over the country." I said and the discussion hovered over a variety of subjects from national to personal. We had had our dinner. It was during this time my orderly entered my room.

"CO Sahib is calling both of you to his room," he announced.

I looked at my watch. It was one in the morning.

"At this hour!" I wondered.

"It must be serious. Or else, the old man would not loss his sleep," said Chouhan. Let's hurry Doc."

The milieu was tense as we reached the office of Col. Rathi. There were Lt. Col Nanda, SP of police Mr. Gehlot and another police officer already in the office. We saluted our CO and took our seats.

"Capt. Nayak, we are at a fix." Col. Rathi was the only one in the battalion who called me by that name instead of the customary Doctor or simply Doc. I was not sure what kind of fix needed to summon for my help.

"Sir, is there anything I can help?" I asked politely.

"The problem is of a sensitive nature," appraised my CO. "You are the only one who can throw some light on this."

I kept quiet. I was not sure where he was leading to.

"You must be aware by this time that we have caught a notorious gangster called Sultan Singh. He is in our custody at present. The police persons wanted to interrogate the man. There is some amount of force to be applied in such cases, as you are aware of. As soon as the interrogation was to start, the man started rolling on the floor on the pretext of having pain in the abdomen. He says that he encounters such pains often, especially when under physical stress. He also says that he has got kidney stones for which he is undergoing treatment. He demands the services of a doctor. Now, we cannot interrogate him on humanitarian grounds as long as it is not clear that he is feigning the illness. If he is not malingering, then he needs some treatment. So your help is required." Col. Rathi looked at me expectantly. "Did he say something about his illness on the way here?" this question was directed to Capt. Chouhan, who swung his head in negative.

"Well Sir," I cleared my throat, "it is not possible for me to say for certain if he is malingering or not. I have to look at his medical documents and maybe we have to take him to the nearby hospital tomorrow for some tests. And if a pain is really there, I can offer some medications for the time being. Can't the interrogation wait till tomorrow?"

"The situation is little tricky there Doctor." It was Mr. Gehlot, the SP who intervened. "This man is a rogue. For different reasons we could not catch hold of him for a long time. He operates a large gang and he is well connected. With his connections higher up in the centre, I am sure we have to let him go within a very short period. I suspect the order from higher up may reach us tomorrow or the day after. Before he is released, we want him to disclose his hideouts and his associates. So we want to utilise whatever time we have at our disposal."

"Our doctor is a smart one and he is sure to find out a way to make sure whether he has the disease or making it up. Give it a try Capt. Nayak." Our CO believed that encouraging one was the best way to bring out his best.

Although inflated by his remarks, I did show not so any sign of it.

"I can give it a try Sir. But I cannot assure of anything. And if he is found to be really ill, then you have to spare him; at least for the time being." I was cautious in my remark.

"That goes without saying," said Gehlot, "we can't violate the human rights of course. Please give it a try."

We came out of the office and I started walking to the room where Sultan Singh was kept captive. The CO and the SP followed. Capt. Chouhan pulled me to a corner to have some words with me. Lt. Thapa, another of our junior officers was there with him.

"Doc! Find out a smart way to detect if he is shamming. I know you can, if you are in your elements." Chouhan pleaded with a diabolic smile on his face.

"Hey! What is your interest?" I asked. "You are not a policeman after all."

"I know," said Thapa, "Chouhan sir took all the trouble in catching the man and he has not been able to try his hands on him yet." Thapa smiled.

I looked at Chouhan scornfully.

"It is not what you think Doc," Chouhan was serious; "I hate the people who keep committing crime and are left out because of their connections. They are worse than our enemies across the border. They are eating up our nation like termites. I don't care whether the police can divulge any information or not. All I like is to bash up the bastard to my heart's content before he is left out of this place. He will think a hundred times before committing another crime."

I knew and admired the patriotism in Chouhan, but that was not the time to ponder over that. I had an intricate problem to tackle with. I gave a call to my nursing assistant and asked him to report in the prisoner's room with the medical bag.

It was quite a scene in the prisoner's room. He was surrounded by a number of uniformed personnel, both police and military. Sultan was curling on a mattress clutching his abdomen with both his hands. "Here comes the Doctor Sahib," someone in the crowd announced. Sultan looked at me expectantly.

"Why don't you sit down, if you can?" I was as polite as with any of my patients.

He looked at me for a second and sat up, leaning on the wall behind. I had a close look at him. Chouhan was right. He was robust, but handsomely built. His height was medium and he had a fair complexion. His thin moustache and trimmed beard went well with his complexion. He looked little over thirty. I wondered how many more crime he would commit when would be set free. Then I looked at the eyes. They were cold and blood shot. I removed my gaze away from his eyes.

"What is the problem you are encountering?" I asked him.

"Look Doctor, I have this problem of stone in kidney since long. I want to be taken to my personal doctor. He is seeing me since quite some time." There was a definite lack of respect in his voice which I disliked. Yet I kept my cool.

"I am afraid that will not be possible at present," I said. "How can you be so sure about your disease? Was it proved by some investigation?"

"Yes, they did the X-ray and ultrasound before confirming the diagnosis. I have to take shots of Baralgan from time to time to keep it in control," he confirmed.

He is using the correct medical terms, I thought. *How can he know all these if he is not a patient himself?* Then I suddenly remembered that he was a lawyer. Lawyers are acquainted with some medical terminologies to handle their cases. Then maybe he used this ploy whenever he was in troubles like this! It was easier for an educated person to remember these terms. So the doubt of him being a malingerer crept in again. There was no definite way to know this. Our medical set up in a battalion level was too small to come to terms with such complications. I looked at the crowd surrounding me. They were watching the developments with interest. I thought hard. Then an idea occurred to me.

"Did you say your pain subsides by shot of Baralgan?" I asked Sultan. Baralgan was a common anti-spasmodic drug that was in use those days.

"Yes, it does," he said, twisting his lips in pain.

"Okay, you seem to be in great pain. We have got injection of Baralgan with us. I will push the drug intravenously to you so that your pain subsides within minutes." I looked straight into his eyes in the gentlest manner possible.

He surveyed me with his cold stare for a moment. It was difficult to fathom his thoughts. Finally he relented, "Alright, push the drug in."

Pritam Singh, my elderly nursing assistant was standing in a corner with the medical bag. "Pritam, load an ampoule of Baralgan in a syringe." I ordered loudly. Then I went closer to him and whispered, "Load 2 ml of Vitamin B-complex instead."

Pritam was an intelligent man and nodded. He pulled 2ml of the vitamin and announced, "I have made the Baralgan ready for use, Sir."

This injectable vitamin resembles the colour of Baralgan being the similar shade of yellow. I showed the syringe to Sultan and said, "Is this the drug your doctor uses regularly on you?"

He nodded.

"So, here we go my friend," I said ceremoniously, "your pain will be relieved in no time." With these words I pushed the drug slowly into his arm vein.

I waited by Sultan's side for his next reaction. After five minutes or so he said, "Now I feel much better." He sat up comfortably on his mattress. "Now, are you convinced that I have the disease? Please hand me over to my doctor the first thing in the morning."

I had a sly smile on my face. "On the other hand, I am going to hand you over to these people around you," I indicated the crowd around us. Then I said to my CO, "The culprit is all yours. He is feigning his illness. I never gave him any pain killer at all. All I injected in his arm was a plain vitamin, which does not have any effect in relieving pain."

The uniformed men jumped over him in unison and interrogation started amidst bouts of manhandling. A free thrashing session was on. I came out of the room. Before I did so, I heard Sultan shouting, "I will see you all, you bastards. You can't keep me here for long. None of you are going to be spared."

The next day, I was congratulated by all for my smartness. But I was not very sure of myself. It was by no means a full proof conclusion that I had come into. There was the possibility that it was a psychological relief on the part of the person thinking the medicine was indeed the one he was used to. As a doctor, I knew this to happen. Then, colicky pain has its periods of remission and at that point it could have been a temporary period of remission only. But at an age of twenty-five I was more interested in savouring the period of glory rather than pondering over the real condition of the patient.

True to Sultan Singh's statement, order to release him came from some big gun at Delhi the next evening. Till that time the police was unable to extract any useful information from him. He had to be released off the custody. The top men of Police and Army kept looking at Sultan Singh in dismay and helplessness as he stepped out of the campus with proud steps and spat on the ground in disdain. Thanks to our democracy!

In the Armed Forces, people are not much concerned about the aftermath of such incidents. Sultan Singh was caught on behest of the Police and was left on orders from higher up. They believe in following orders and in direct action. Sultan, even if discussed occasionally may be over the dinner table, no serious thought was given to him. Over a period, his memory became fade to me as well. One month had passed since the Sultan Singh episode. Punjab was coming back to its normal life fast. Though we were not encouraged to socialise with the civilians, I had to meet a few doctors in the local hospital because of the nature of my duty. One of them, Dr. GS Sodhi got very friendly to me. His house was adjacent to the college campus where we had camped. In spite of his repeated invitations to visit his house I kept avoiding the invitation. But on one occasion, I had to relent. It was his daughter's fifth birthday. I was called for dinner. I approached my CO.

"Capt. Nayak," he frowned, "we, the forces people do not like to mingle with the civilians as such. In spite of the tension having been relaxed to a large extent, I still feel apprehensive. But since you have accepted the invitation, I will certainly not allow you to be dishonoured." He was a hard core military man.

As I thanked him, he asked me to take a jeep along with two armed soldiers.

"That will not be necessary, Sir," I told him, "the doctor's house is nearby. It takes only five minutes by walking."

"Okay, don't take a vehicle. But I will insist on taking two armed personnel with you."

Going to a private birthday party with armed guards was uncomfortable, to say the least. Yet I did not have any other way. I slipped into a civil dress and took my armed companions with me. It was a spectacle! Me, a most ordinary mortal, being escorted by two carbine wielding soldiers! I felt embarrassed. In fact, I cursed the way with the Army. I was from a civilian back ground and sometimes I felt the Army ways to be a bit overbearing. But a little bit later I realised how foresighted our CO was.

We had to take a little detour to reach Dr. Sodhi's place while going through the front gate of the campus. We took a narrow lane on the way. It was about six in the evening. The surrounding was visible clearly. On our way the sessions court fell to our left. In spite of the court having been closed, there were a number of people strolling in front of it. Few black clad lawyers were also in view. Then I spotted one in the crowd. In fact, I had to spot him. It was our Sultan Singh! The handsome man in white trouser and black coat was throwing a steely stare at me with his hands tucked on his waist. He was within ten feet from us, standing with two other persons; possibly his clients. I could see his eyes distinctly. They were cold and evil to the core as usual and were following every step of mine. I remembered Chouhan. A wave of chill ran though my spine. I wondered what could be my condition sans the two guards of mine. Yet I kept a brave face and maintained my normal pace. On the turn of the lane I looked back again. Sultan had turned round and kept his vigil on me. However, on my journey back through the same lane, there was no sign of Sultan Singh.

I am a simple fellow. Virtues like bravery and physical strength are not my forte. My background is middleclass and I had joined the Armed Forces more out of need than because of patriotism or love for adventure. A few days after that, our battalion came back from Kapurthala and I opted for a release from the forces few years following that. These are the things of long past now. Sometimes I still wonder whether Sultan Singh was really malingering or not. And those eyes of him! They still haunt me in an occasional nightmare. My firm belief is he does not remember me anymore. He must have more important matters to be taken care of.

Still, as a precautionary measure, I have never ventured to visit Kapurthala again till this day.